Future Imperfect

A thoughtful young man sat down to write this novel in 1950. The novel is set in the future, but its timeless theme has to do with the possible wellsprings of the random wars and killings that occupied men's souls at that time, as they do today and probably will when you are gone.

In these pages, composed a generation ago, endless peace talks go on in the city of Paris; Russians and Asians quarrel about the orbits of their spy satellites; and the American people are hooked on a soft drink that mysteriously expands and heightens the emotions—and is as easy to buy as cream soda.

But forecasts of possible future phenomena are only incidental. Like all of John D. MacDonald's novels, it is a masterfully told story about believable people and the events that shape their lives.

The Wine has aged very well.

WINE OF THE
DREAMERS

JOHN D. MacDONALD

A FAWCETT GOLD MEDAL BOOK

Fawcett Publications, Inc., Greenwich, Conn.
Member of American Book Publishers Council, Inc.

ONE

THE SOFT PURR OF THE TURBINE WAS ALMOST LOST IN the roar of wind as the gray sedan traveled south through the New Mexico night. The night air, as always, was cool. Night in this land, he thought, is different. The land seems to rest from the heavy fist of the sun.

Step out of the cool shadows of early morning and the sun is a vast white blow between the eyes. The sun sucks greedily at all liquids. A man lost for a full day in the wastes of rock and sand will be found in the blue dusk, curled in fetal position, lips black, body withered and mummified like the long-dead.

Parched, wind-driven air dries the membranes of mouth and nose. The sun gaunts the men, pinches wrinkles into the flesh around the eyes. It fades colors and drabs the women.

At night, in the blue desert dusk the jukes sing out the plaintive old ballads, and the young girls dance with a determined abandon. For the young girls know that the sun makes short work of youth, and juices are soon gone. Flat bronzed Indian faces look in at the dancers, and their eyes are polished obsidian. They know that they alone are bred for this land, and when the pallid laughing ones are gone, they will remain.

There are racial memories, more of a faint pulse of blood and ache of bone than a true memory. The sun is a god. The god is angered because the tall pyramids are no longer used. The sun has long since baked away the faint stains on the pyramid crests, on the stone bowls, the time-worn channels. At dawn the sun hears no chant, sees no black upraised glint of stone knife, sees no

5

blinded virgin awaiting the clever twisting thrust that rips the pulsing heart from its hot membranous nest.

Maybe, he thought, big hands resting easily on the wheel as he drove, they are closer to truth than we are. We and our learned talk of hydrogen-helium reaction.

Speed at night was a hypnotic. The speedometer needle held steady at ninety-five. Faint vibration from the road surface. White onrushing flick of an insect caught in the hard bright headlight beams. And weariness. Bard Lane knew that his weariness was of a very special type. An all-inclusive type, compounded of physical, intellectual and emotional strain, each carried to the threshold of tolerance. For a moment the car seemed to be standing still while the road ahead leaped toward him and was snatched under the wheels. He bunched his shoulders, shook his head violently to thrust back the impulse toward sleep that for a moment had brushed his eyelids. He adjusted the side vent a bit to throw a stronger current of the cool air against his face.

Far ahead the Christmas tree of a truck appeared, heading in the same direction. He came up on it slowly, made a pass signal with his lights and swept by, noting that it was a truck train, with heavy quad trailers. Once by the truck he sat a bit higher in the seat so that he could use the rearview mirror and the diminishing glow of the truck lights to check on the prisoner who slept curled on the back seat.

Far ahead he saw the lights of a lonesome town. He diminished speed gradually, saw the single traffic light ahead turn from green to red. In the glow of the lights along the deserted sidewalks, he glanced at the girl who slept beside him. She had slumped over toward the door so that her head appeared to be uncomfortably braced in the angle between door and seat back. Long legs were stretched out under the dash, and both hands, palms up, fingers curled, rested in her lap. She looked remarkably young and quite helpless. Bard Lane knew that there was nothing at all helpless about Sharan Inly. At the southern outskirts of the town he picked up speed again, and felt the heaviness of eyelids begin anew.

He shook his head again, reached out and punched one of the radio buttons, turning the volume down so as not to disturb the girl.

". . . and remember, when you're bored, drink Wilkins' Mead, spelled em ee aye dee. Wilkins' Mead is non-alcoholic, non-habitforming. Four out of five doctors know that Wilkins' Mead cures boredom through a simple process of intensifying your reception to all stimuli. Three years ago, in May of 1972, Wilkins' Mead was placed on the market. Since that time, one hundred and sixty million Americans have learned that you have never really seen a sunset, enjoyed a kiss, tasted a steak until you have first had your handy lip-sized bottle of Wilkins' Mead. And now for your Wilkins' Mead reporter, the man the Senate couldn't silence, Melvin C. Lynn, with his nightly Wilkins' Mead summary of news of the world. . . ."

"This is Melvin C. Lynn, reporting the news for Wilkins' Mead and the Wilkins Laboratories, where the secret of your happiness was developed.

"This has been a quiet day on the international front. The Paris Conference continues and an informed source stated late this afternoon that the delegates have not yet lost hope of reaching an agreement on the basic problems confronting them. The Pan-Asia delegate has flown back to Moscow for further instructions on the Siberian agreement not to launch snooper satellites until new orbits have been assigned to each major power. The South American Coalition has refused to back down on their claim to five thousand miles of their moon base, even though they admit that it is almost a month since the last weak signals were received, and all expedition personnel must be assumed dead. Tomorrow, and throughout the world, as well as at the conference, there will be the customary sixty seconds of silence to commemorate the anniversary of the loss of the first manned rocket to Mars . . .

"And now for the national news front. Bliss Bailey, the Staten Island ferry boat captain who barricaded the ferry-boat bridge and chugged off toward Bermuda, was brought back under guard today. The commuters who took the inadvertent cruise with Captain Bailey have reported that once it was discovered that the ferryboat was heading east across a calm sea and nothing could be done, most of them turned it into a holiday. The identity of the nude blonde who jumped overboard the first night out has not yet been discovered. Bailey is quoted as saying, 'It just seemed like a good idea at the time.' Witnesses say Bailey appeared slightly dazed. His employers have not yet made public their decision regarding Captain Bailey. His cruise passengers are circulating a petition for his reemployment.

"Well, tomorrow morning the new slot-machine divorce law goes into effect in Nevada. Thirty machines have been installed to handle the expected rush of business. Applicants will slide a fifty-dollar bill into the waiting slot, then give their name, address and reason for requesting a divorce in a clear, low voice into the mike, then press their right thumb firmly against the exposed sensitive plate. Six weeks later they will return to the same machine and duplicate the procedure and the decree will fall into the hopper.

"Speaker of the House, Wally Blime, was severely reprimanded today in the public press and over the airwaves. This reporter feels, as others do after yesterday's childish display, that bubble gum and a pea shooter are rather poor substitutes for the dignity expected of a public figure in high office. Blime's only defense is that 'Something told me to do it.' And this, my friends, is from the same man who, two years ago, broke fourteen windows on New York's Madison Avenue before he was restrained by the police. His defense, at that time, was the same. Wally, this is a word from a friend. This reporter feels that it is high time you returned to private life.

"Larry Roy, national TV favorite, today jumped or fell from the forty-first story of a New York City hotel. Melly

Muro, Larry Roy's seventh wife, told police that she could think of no reason for suicide, unless it could be a breakdown due to overwork. Melly, you will remember, is the redheaded woman who figured so largely in the divorce of Franz Steeval, composer and conductor, three months ago. Larry Roy was her sixth husband.

"Martha Needis, the Jersey City landlady who, last Tuesday, murdered her six roomers in their beds with a steak tenderizer, is still at large.

"In Memphis, debutante Gayla Dennison was today acquitted of murdering her guardian. She wept tears of joy.

"At Aberdeen Proving Ground in Maryland, government psychiatrists today disagreed on their diagnoses in the case of Corporal Brandt Reilly, the enlisted man who, ten days ago, turned an aircraft cannon on a company formation, killing sixteen and wounding twenty-one.

"And here is a light note in the news. Today, Pierre Brevet, French artist, is in serious danger of being lynched by irate American womanhood. He has been in this country for three days. He told reporters that he heartily approves, for French women, the new beachwear consisting of halters only, but after a visit to Jones Beach yesterday, he feels that this is one daring style this country could do without. He stated that his objections are deep-seated. Could that be a pun, Pierre?"

"You have just heard Melvin C. Lynn with the Wilkins' Mead news. And now do you hear that? Know what it is? You—pouring your first full golden glass of Wilkins' Mead from its handy lip-sized bottle. And tonight you have that date you've been waiting for. The big important date with the 'one and only.' Take her a bottle of Wilkins' Mead too. And then you can be sure that the two of you will enjoy one of the most——"

Bard Lane grunted and punched at the radio button. The airdale voice was mercifully silenced.

Sharan Inly said wryly, "No mead for me. But a beer would go good, if the man can arrange it."

"Did I wake you up with that racket? Sorry."

"You didn't wake me up. That creamy little voice of Melvin C.'s is insidious. It crept into my dreams, licking its chops at sudden death, Bard. I listen to him and feel that we're in an age of decay, and he is its prophet. Wonder what compulsion makes him go all oily over a nice juicy hammer murder?"

"You work all the time, don't you, Sharan? Always the psychiatrist."

He could feel her eyes on him. "You always shy away from psychiatry. There's always a little bitterness in your voice when you bring it up. Why?"

"If I start telling you my attitude, it will turn into an argument. Looks like a beer spot ahead. How's our boy?"

She knelt on the front seat and reached into the back as he began to slow for the neon flicker far ahead. She turned and plumped down into the seat with a sigh. "He'll keep for another three hours without a booster shot. Better park where it isn't too light, so nobody will get nosey."

There were a few shining new cars in the large parking lot, a larger number of dusty heaps, some pickup trucks and a few huge trans-state trucks. Bard parked near a weary-looking clump of live oaks, and carefully locked the car. He straightened up and stretched stiffness out of his joints. Sharan, standing nearby, made the time-honored and infinitely feminine gesture of looking back down over each shoulder to see how badly her skirt was wrinkled. The night breeze molded the thin skirt against the long clean thigh-lines, the trim hips. He felt the stir of pleasure in looking at her, along with the knowledge of the trap. Biological trap. Nature takes clear fresh skin, and youth and a slim body, and the child-bearing ability, holds it up and says, "This is what you want." And the pulse responds.

The acid twang of a jukebox cowhand quavered on the night air. ". . . *She never reely tole me that she loved meeeee . . .*"

There were metal tables on the patio, on the stones that were still warm underfoot from the sun-heat of the long day. He held a chair for Sharan, then went inside, walking the cramped tiredness out of his legs, muffling a yawn with the back of his hand.

Inside there were booths and dancers and girl-laughter and soft drinks held under the table edge for the quick jolt from the package store bottle. He stood at the beer bar and waited patiently, a tall tanned man with blunt bones in his face, with widow's peak slanting sharply back into the crisp brown hair, gray-touched, with an odd look that combined both mildness and authority. He wore a rumpled khaki hunting jacket over a faded blue work shirt, open at the throat.

He carried the two frosted bottles and one glass out to the table. Sharan was making up her lips, turned in the chair so the light from the doorway struck her mirror at the right angle. She smiled up at him, capped the lipstick and dropped it back into her white purse.

"How are we running on time, Bard?"

"We can kill a half hour and still get there a good hour before the conference."

"Want me to drive for a while?"

"No thanks. It's better to be doing something."

His big brown fist rested on the table top. She patted it with a quick, affectionate gesture. "Don't let it get you down. Screening wasn't your responsibility."

"My responsibility is to get the job done. I couldn't pass the buck if I wanted to."

The light behind her haloed her cropped curls. She was indeed pleasant to look at. A face that was almost, but not quite, thin—with eagerness, mobility, sensitivity. She held her glass in both hands, like a child. Thrown together on the job, they had kept their relationship on the plane of friendship, mutual respect. There had been isolated moments—bending together over a desk, a quick glance across a crowded office, an inadvertent touch—when he had become conscious of his own awareness, and hers. But by unspoken agreement between them they always forced a return to an unemotional status. Maybe one day there would be time. Maybe one day the pressure of responsibility would be taken away, and there would be time for play.

He had wondered about her in the beginning. This new crop of young professional women no longer had any consciousness of fighting for equality. It existed. In the beginning he had accepted the idea that her amorality would be no less casual than that of the other women her age on the project. For a time he had skirted the idea of asking her to add the self-evident closer aspect to their association. But, at the time, he had decided that his duty was to maintain all his energies at the highest possible peak.

Now he was glad he had made that decision, for as he had come to know her better he realized that a casual amorality would not integrate with the rest of her character. In fact, she would probably be decidedly old-fashioned in that regard. And, had he asked her bluntly, he suspected that something in their relationship would have ceased to exist in the moment she denied him.

Women who played for keeps were becoming so rare as to be refreshing.

Until the all-pervading, all-important, capital J Job was done, Sharan Inly would remain Dr. Inly, Project Assistant in Charge of Psycho-Adjustment.

"The General," she said dolefully, "is going to be *muy irritado.*"

"That is an understatement. Fat blue sparks are going to crackle off his fingertips."

She finished her glass, refilled it from the bottle. "How about that argument we're going to have? Want to start now?"

"You want to hear someone attack your profession, Dr. Inly?"

"Sure. I'm a missionary. I'll bring enlightenment to your poor layman mind."

"Here goes. Ever since Freud and Jung, you people have been honing certain basic weapons. I am a layman in psychiatry. However, I am a scientist. As a scientist, I am disturbed by your acceptance of the truth of your basic assumptions. Take the case of the critter we've got out in the car. I'll use a little of your gobbledegook language. He's been screened two ways. Loyalty and, in your province, stability. You hunted for all the garden-variety neuroses and couldn't find any of any importance. Ergo, we've got a stable guy. No delusions of persecution, no manic-depressive tendencies, no control so excessive it smells of dementia praecox. Doesn't miss his mother, save lady's shoes or draw pornographic pictures. Your ink-blot tests, properly fitted into statistical distribution charts, show that Mr. X is a nice clean-living ambiverent, ideal technician material."

She frowned. "You quarrel with that?"

"Not at all. But the neat little tests assume that this stability is a permanent state."

"They do not! The tests and the whole theory admit that in the face of unexpected strain, even the most stable, the most adjusted, can become psychoneurotic in one way or another. My goodness, that's why I'm employed out there. It's my job to detect the presence of any change in the face of strain and . . ."

"Now you're stating my point. I say that one of your basic assumptions is that there has to be an environmental change to create the strain which results in an alteration of this basic quotient of stability. I say that the assumption is too hasty. I say that there is something further to study. I think the shift from stability to instability can come in the twinkling of an eye and come without reference to any outside stimuli. Forget hereditary weaknesses. Forget the old business about escaping from a life that is unbearable. I say that you can take a perfectly adjusted guy, put him in a situation where his life is satisfying—and boom, he can go off like that. You've seen it. I've seen it. Why? Why does it happen? It happened to Bill Kornal. One minute he was okay. The next minute it was as though something . . . quite *alien* took over his mind. So now we've got him out in the car and there's four month's work lost."

"Are we going to go back, Bard, to the old idea of being possessed by devils?"

"Maybe we should. How about the news we listened to? What keeps perpetually messing up mankind? Jokers who go off their rocker when they've got every reason not to. No, you people are doing a good, but a limited job. Floating around somewhere is an X factor that you haven't found yet. Until you do I'm looking at psychology and psychiatry with a limited and dubious acceptance, Sharan."

There was a whisper of sound. He searched the night sky until he saw, against the stars, the running lights of a jet transport, losing altitude for the Albuquerque landing, the six flame-tongues merged, by the altitude, into a thin orange line.

The breeze stirred her hair. She said slowly, "I should rise up in mighty wrath and smite you hip and thigh, boss. But a still small voice within me says there might be something in what you say. However, if I admit you might be right, I'm also admitting the impossibility of ever isolating this X factor. How can you find something that hits without warning and disappears the same way?"

"Possession by devils," he said, grinning.

She stood up, slim against the light, more provocative to him in her complete, thoughtful, forgetfulness of self than if she had posed carefully.

"Then," she said, "the devils are more active lately. Oh, I know that every generation that reaches middle age believes firmly that the world is going to hell. But this time, Bard, even at my tender years, I think they may have something. Our culture seems like a big machine that's vibrating itself to bits. Parts keep flying off. Parts that are important. Decency, dignity, morality. We've all gone impulsive. Anything you want to do is all right, provided your urge is strong enough. It's a . . . a . . ."

"Sociological anarchy?"

"Yes. And there, Mr. Lane, you have my motivation. Now you know why I'm so desperately anxious for you to succeed. I keep feeling that if mankind can find some new horizons, there'll be a return to a decent world. Quaint, aren't I?"

They walked across the lot toward the car. He looked at the night sky, at the stars which seemed closer, more attainable here.

"Elusive devils, aren't they?"

She caught his wrist as they walked, her nails biting into the flesh with quick strength. "They won't stay elusive, Bard. They *won't.*"

"Four years now, that I've had my little obsession, Sharan, and they seem as far away as ever."

"You'll never give up, Bard."

"I wonder."

They had reached the car. Through the rear window, open an inch, came the soft sound of Bill Kornal's snores.

"It makes me feel ill to have you talk of giving up," she said in a half-whisper.

He leaned over to put the key in the lock. His shoulder brushed hers.

Without quite knowing how it had happened, he found her in his arms. She stood tightly against him with up-turned lips, and with a small, plaintive sound in her throat. He knew that he was bruising her mouth, and could not stop. He knew it was a forgetfulness, a little time stolen from the project, from the endless drain of effort and responsibility. He had expected to find in her all the warmth and passion of any healthy young adult. He was pleased that her intensity matched his own.

"This is no good," she said.

She stood a little aside, her head bent. He knelt and swept his hand back and forth across the gravel until he found the keys. He straightened up.

"Sorry," he said.

"We're both tired, Bard. We're both scared to death of what General Sachson might do. We were clinging to each other for . . . comfort. Let's forget it."

"Let's not exactly forget it, Sharan. Let's shelve it for future action."

"Please," she said sharply.

"All right, so I shouldn't have said that." He knew that his tone was a shade indignant.

He unlocked the door. She slid under the wheel and across to her side. He chunked the door shut and drove out in a long curve onto the highway, accelerated viciously up to cruising speed. He gave her a quick glance. She was staring straight ahead, her face expressionless in the reflected dash lights. A big jack bounded from the shoulder into the road, startling him. He felt the tiny thud in his wrists as the wheel hit it, heard her sharp intake of breath.

"Just say I was possessed by one of those devils," he said.

"Probably we both were," she said. He glanced again and saw her smile. She moved a bit closer to him. "Besides, Bard, I'm a prim kid, I guess."

"Didn't taste very prim."

"That's what I mean," she said, enigmatically. "Now be good."

The gray sedan droned through the night.

TWO

AS THE GRAYNESS IN THE EAST BEGAN TO PALE THE conference room lighting, Bard and Sharan sat with the other three persons awaiting General Sachson.

Gray, shaggy Colonel Powys, Projects Coordinator, rolled a yellow octagonal pencil against the polished top of the conference table, pressing so hard with his palm that the pencil made an irritating clacking sound as it rolled. Major Leeber, Sachson's aide, sleek and demurely pompous, nibbled at one edge of his moustache. The lean enlisted stenotype clerk turned a glass ashtray around and around and around.

Bard glanced over at Sharan. She gave him a wan smile. There were bluish shadows around her eyes.

"The general's very upset about this," Powys rumbled. His words dropped, like stones, into the pool of silence. There was an accusation behind his tone. The inference was that no one else was upset. Bard Lane restrained the impulse toward sarcasm.

The wall clock had a sweep second hand. Each time the hand made one full revolution, the minute hand jumped one notch with a tiny grating clack. Leeber yawned like a sated cat. He said, in a soft voice, "You're quite young for all that responsibility, Dr. Inly."

"Too young, Major?" Sharan asked politely.

"You're putting words in my mouth, Doctor."

"Major, I use that prefix for state occasions. I am Miss Inly."

He smiled at her, sleepy-lidded.

As the sweep second hand touched the hour and the minute hand clacked, the door swung open and General Sachson came in, small blue eyes full of electric crackle, neat heels striking at the rug. He was of minimum stature for Army requirements, with a face like a dried butternut, a man of snap and spit and polish and a score of uniforms tailored by experts.

"Hen *shut!*" Powys brayed. Only Sharan remained seated.

Sachson rounded the corner of the table, flicked his eyes across them in the moment of silence and then sat down, indicating with a chopping gesture of a child's thin brown hand that they should do the same.

"Meeting to order!" he snapped. "For God's sake, Sergeant, get the names right this time."

"Yes sir," the sergeant said in an utterly uninflected voice.

"Report damage, Dr. Lane. And keep to the point."

"Kornal broke down the door of the lab where the control panels were being assembled. He was alone in there for an estimated ten minutes. Adamson estimates that Kornal set us back four full months."

"I assume," Sachson said in a deceptively mild tone, "that the door was not considered sufficiently important to be guarded."

"There were two guards. Kornal knocked them down with a piece of pipe. One is all right. The other is in danger. A depressed skull fracture."

"The military, Dr. Lane, has discovered that the use of a password is not exactly a childish device."

"Kornal was privileged to secure a pass at any time to enter that lab. He was working long hours."

Sachson let the silence grow. The sergeant sat with his waiting fingers poised on the stenotype keys. The blue eyes swung slowly around to Sharan Inly.

"As I understand the theory of your work, Dr. Inly, it is your responsibility to anticipate any mental or emotional breakdown, is it not?" Sachson asked. His tone was replete with the mock gallantry which showed his distaste for the involvement of women in such projects as the one at hand.

Bard Lane saw Sharan's pallor increase a bit. "As William Kornal had access to all portions of the project area, General, it is self-evident that he was a double A risk on a psychological basis."

Sachson's smile was thin-lipped. "Possibly I am stupid, Dr. Inly. I don't find things to be as 'self-evident' as you seem to think they are."

"He was given a routine check three days ago, General."

"Possibly the error, Dr. Inly, is in applying so-called routine methods to special cases. Just what *is* a routine check?"

"A hypnotic is administered and the employee is asked a series of questions about his work. His answers are compared with the answers he gave on all previous checks. If there is any deviation—any deviation whatsoever—then the more exhaustive special investigation is instigated."

"You can prove, of course, that Kornal was actually given this routine check?"

Sharan blushed. "Am I to consider that a question, General?"

"Forgive me, Dr. Inly. I am a very blunt man. I have seen post-dated reports before. It merely occurred to me that——"

"I can back up Dr. Inly on that, if you feel she needs proof," Bard said in a harsh voice.

The blue eyes flicked over toward Bard. "I prefer, Dr. Lane, to have my questions answered by the person to whom they are directed. It saves confusion in the records of the meeting." He turned back to Sharan. "Why are not all the tests special rather than routine?"

"They could be, General, if my staff were tripled and if the persons to be tested were relieved of all project duty for a three-day period."

"That would build up quite an empire for you, Dr. Inly."

Sharan's eyes narrowed. "General, I am perfectly willing to answer your questions. I realize that somehow I should have anticipated Kornal's violent aberration. I do not know how I could have, but I know I should have. I accept that blame. But I do not have to accept innuendos regarding any possible dishonesty on my part, or any desire on my part to make myself more important."

"Strike that out of the record, Sergeant," Sachson snapped.

"I would prefer to have it remain in the record," she said quietly.

Sachson looked down at his small brown hands. He sighed. "If you feel that the record of this meeting is inadequate, you are privileged to write a letter to be attached to all copies that go forward from this headquarters. So long as I conduct these meetings, I shall direct the preparation of the minutes. Is that quite clear?"

"Yes sir," Powys said quickly, sitting at attention in his chair.

"Sergeant," Sachson said. "Kindly stop tapping on that thing. This will be off the record. I wish to say that I have had a reasonably successful military career. It has been successful because I have consistently avoided all those situations where I could have been given responsibility without authority. Now I am faced with just such a situation. For any ranking officer, it is a death trap. I do not like it. I cannot give you orders, Dr. Lane. I can only make suggestions. Each time you fall further behind schedule, it affects my record, my two-oh-one file, my military reputation. You civilians have no way of knowing what that means. You can switch bosses. Things are forgotten, or overlooked. I always answer to the same boss. There are always Siberias to which an officer can be sent."

"Isn't this project considerably more important than any one man's reputation?" Bard asked, hearing Powys' shocked in-suck of breath.

"That, Dr. Lane," Sachson said, "is a pretty ethereal point of view. Let me tell you exactly what I think of Project Tempo. On all previous extraterrestrial projects, the armed forces have been in complete control. Civilian specialists have been employed on a civil service basis in a technical and advisory capacity. Our appropriations have been part of general military appropriations. And, I might add, those projects which I was privileged to command were all completed on or ahead of schedule.

"Now, Dr. Lane, you are in command, if I may use that word. You have the authority. I have the responsibility. It is a damnable situation. I know far too little of what is going on up in your hidden valley in the Sangre de Cristo Mountains. I know that a properly run guard detail, along military lines, would have prevented this . . . this accident. Now I am making this request of you. As soon as we start talking for the minutes again, you will ask me to detail Major Leeber to the project area in an advisory capacity. Major Leeber will report directly to me on all matters which, in his good judgment, may tend to endanger the promptness of completion of the contract."

Bard Lane tensed at the threat hidden behind the words. "And if I object?"

"I have given this considerable thought, Dr. Lane. If you object, I shall ask to be relieved of all future responsibility in connection with Project Tempo. That will, of course, make a stink. It will be wafted to the nostrils of our lawmakers. Already there is some discernible pressure for a senate committeee to investigate this project and the apparently endless number of dollars required. My resignation will crystallize that move. You and your project will be investigated."

"And?" Bard Lane said softly.

"And you will find that many people in Washington, many important people, will have the same idea that I have: the only way to deep space, my scientific friend, is through further perfections in physical propulsion units, such as the current A-six tubes. All this Einsteinian space fold, time field stuff is so much dreaming."

"If you're so certain of that, General, why don't you recommend that the project be discontinued?"

"That is no part of my responsibility. My responsibility is to get your ship, the Beatty One, off the ground. If it fails in flight, it is no reflection on me. If you can't get it off the ground, we can use the hull for a military project now under consideration. You have your choice, Dr. Lane. Cooperate in the matter of my assigning Leeber, or reconcile yourself to giving up the project."

Bard Lane took long seconds to organize his thinking. He said, "General, let me be presumptuous enough to summarize recent history of interplanetary travel. Ever since initial work on the old chemical propulsion V-two at White Sands over twenty-five years ago, it has been a history of failure. Those failures can be divided into three categories. One—technical deficiencies in staff and the ships. Two—espionage and sabotage. Three—weaknesses in the human factor.

"Project Tempo, General, has its own answer to each category of failure. Placing full authority in the civilian technical staff is the answer to category one. Secret location and careful loyalty screening is the answer to two. Dr. Inly and her staff are the answer to three. I am still in command, as you say. I will take Major Leeber under three conditions. One—he will not discuss technical problems or theory with any member of the staff. Two—he will wear civilian clothes and conform to all rules. Three —he will submit to class A security clearance, and to an extended stability test given all new employees."

Leeber flushed and stared at the ceiling.

Sachson said, "Dr. Lane, do you feel you are in any position to set up those restrictions?"

Bard knew that this was the focal point of the entire meeting. If he backed down Leeber would soon acquire his own staff, a nucleus of a military headquarters, and inch by inch General Sachson would take over control. If he did not back down, Sachson might do as he threatened. Yet such a resignation would not look well on the general's record.

"I will not accept Major Leeber on any other basis," Dr. Lane said.

Sachson stared at him for a full ten seconds. He sighed. "I see no reason not to meet you halfway, Doctor. I do resent the implication that any member of my personal staff might be a poor security risk."

"General, I can remember the case of Captain Sangerson," Bard reminded him gently.

Sachson appeared not to have heard. He looked at Leeber. "Get the prisoner, Major," he said.

Leeber opened the conference room door and spoke softly to the guard. Bill Kornal was brought in immediately.

Sharan Inly gasped and hurried to his side, examined the purple swelling under Kornal's left eye. She turned toward the General, her brown eyes suddenly brittle. "This man is a patient, not a prisoner, General. Why has he been struck?"

Kornal grinned miserably. "Don't make an issue of it, Dr. Inly. I don't blame the guy who clobbered me."

"Strike that off the record, Sergeant," Sachson said. "Take that chair, Kornal. You are—or were—a technician."

"More than a technician," Bard Lane said quickly. "Kornal is a competent physicist with over five years at Brookhaven."

"I'll accept that," Sachson said. His eyes were cool. "But it shouldn't be necessary to keep reminding you, Dr. Lane, that I wish answers from the person addressed." He turned his attention back to Kornal. "You smashed delicate equipment. Do you know the penalties for willful destruction of government property?"

"That isn't important," Kornal said bleakly.

General Sachson smiled. "I consider that to be a very peculiar statement. Possibly you can explain it to me."

"General," Kornal said, "the Beatty One means more to me than I could explain to you. I've never worked harder for anything in my life. And I was never happier. I don't care if the punishment is boiling in oil."

"You have a strange way of expressing your great regard for Project Tempo. Maybe you can tell us why you destroyed government property."

"I don't know."

"Possibly you don't want to tell us who employed you to smash the panels?" Sachson said in a silky voice.

"All I can do is tell you the way I told Bar——Dr. Lane, General. I woke up and couldn't get back to sleep. I put my clothes on and went out for some air and a smoke. I was standing outside when all of a sudden the cigarette fell out of my hand. Like somebody took over my hand and opened the fingers. Like I was being pushed back into a little corner of my mind, where I could look out, but I couldn't do anything."

"Hypnotized, I suppose," Sachson said acidly.

"I don't know. It wasn't like when they give you that hypnotic drug. My own mind wasn't fogged up. Just shoved back into a corner. That's the only way I can describe it."

"So there you were with your mind in a corner. Continue, please."

"I went over to where the carpenters had been putting up a new bunkhouse. The plumbers had left some lengths of pipe around. I picked up a short length and shoved it inside my belt. Then I went over to the lab and walked up to the two guards. They knew me. All this time you've got to understand, my body was doing things without my mind telling it to. And I had the funny feeling, sort of on the *edge* of my mind, that it wasn't right to be building the Beatty One. It was nasty, somehow. Dirty. And all my friends, all the people sleeping in the area, they were enemies and not . . . very bright. You know what I mean?"

Sachson stared at him. "I think that needs a little more explanation."

Kornal scratched his head. "Look. Suppose you went into an African village at night, General. They were all asleep. You would feel a lot smarter and superior to those savages, General, and yet you might be a little afraid of them waking up and ganging up on you. It was like that. I pulled out the pipe and hit the two guards, backhand and forehand. They dropped and I broke the door down. I went in, and it was like I'd never been there before. The equipment, the panels and all, they weren't familiar to me. They were dirty, like the Beatty One, and I had to smash them. I had ten minutes in there before they got me. As soon as they grabbed me, I was myself again. I did a good job in there. Adamson cried when he saw it. Cried like a baby. The thing that took over my mind and body . . . it was a kind of devil, I guess."

Bard intercepted Sharan's quick, startled look.

"The devils had you, eh?" Sachson said, his eyebrows arching up toward his hairline in mock astonishment.

"Something had me. Something walked in and took over. There wasn't a single damn thing I could do about it, either. After I was myself again, I tried to kill myself. But I couldn't do it."

Sachson turned to Colonel Powys. "What's S.O.P., on such cases, Roger."

Powys had a rusty, rumbling voice. "We can't bring it to trial, General, if the suspect knows too much about any top secret project still under process of completion.

When that man tried to blow up the Gettysburg Three he had almost the same story this man has. The head doctors thought up a name for it, and we stowed him away in the nut house until the Gettysburg Three took off. Of course she turned unstable at five hundred miles up and crashed off Hawaii——"

"I didn't ask for a history of the Mars flights, Colonel. What happened to McBride?"

"Well, sir, when Gettysburg Three was done for, the head doctors said McBride had recovered and so we brought him to trial. Because he was an enlisted man, we were able to give him five years at hard labor, but as I see it, this Kornal doesn't come under us."

Sachson gave Powys a frigid glare. "Thank you, Colonel. Brief and to the point, as usual."

Bard spoke to Kornal. "Bill, I think you'd better come back on the project. Want to try it?"

"Want to?" He held out his clever hands. "God, how I'd work! Adamson says four months lost. I could cut that down to less than three."

Sachson said harshly, "Are you completely mad, Lane?"

Bard ignored him. "What do you think, Sharan?"

"If he can pass the original psycho-screening tests, I don't see why not. We are using the best tests known. If he can pass them, he should be as acceptable as anyone who can pass them. Major Leeber can take them at the same time."

"I go on record as objecting to this," Sachson said.

"Me too," Powys rumbled.

"Sorry, General," Bard said. "Kornal is a highly trained man. We need him. If this was a temporary aberration, and not part of a repetitive pattern, he can help us undo the harm he did. I haven't time for thinking about fitting punishment to crime. Bill will punish himself more than anyone else ever could."

Sachson stood up. "It seems to be your baby. But it's all in the minutes. When he loses another four months for you, Project Tempo will either be disbanded, or have a new director. Sergeant, Dr. Lane will give you the exact wording on his request for Major Leeber. Meeting adjourned. Take Leeber with you when you drive back."

They stood in silence as the little general strode out of the room, favoring them all with a final bleak nod.

As soon as the door closed behind the general, Major Leeber said unctuously, "I know that you folks are thinking of me as a thorn in your side. It wasn't my fault the Old Man pushed me down your throat. But, believe me, I'll stay out of your way. Tommy Leeber can be a real happy guy. All the boy needs is that five o'clock jolt of firewater and a few shell-pink ears to whisper into. Couple of times a week I'll mail the old man a double-talk report and we can all live happily together in the mountains."

Leeber had a lazy grin on overly-full lips under the dark military moustache, but under sleepy lids his eyes were steady, cold, unwinking black.

"Happy to have you with us," Bard said without warmth.

Sharan stood up. Leeber moved closer to her. "And about you, Miss Inly? Are you glad to have me aboard?"

"Of course," she said absently. "Bard, how soon are we starting back?"

"Better make it noon. That will give some time for a little sleep."

The others left. The sergeant looked expectantly at Bard. Bard smiled at him. "You know your boss. Write it up in any way that will make him happy, just so long as the conditions I imposed are included. Do you have them down?"

"Yes sir. Want me to read them back?"

"No need of that." He walked toward the door.

The sergeant said, "Uh . . . Doctor Lane."

He turned. "Yes?"

"About Major Leeber. He's very smart, Doctor. And he gets along fine in the Army. I think maybe someday he'll be a general."

"A worthy ambition, I suppose."

"He likes to make a . . . good impression, where it counts most."

"Thanks, Sergeant. Thanks very much."

The sergeant grinned. "Mention it not, Doctor."

Back in the room assigned him in the B.O.Q., Bard Lane lay awaiting the steep drop into exhausted sleep. He thought of what Kornal had said. Possession by devils. A devil that could invade the unwilling mind, use the reluctant body as a tool. Were the ancients closer to the truth than we, with our measurements and dials and ink blot tests? A man could not face the theory that there is a measure of built-in instability in the mind, that insanity can come with the next breath. Even a theory of devils is more comforting than that. Maybe, he thought, we share this planet, have always shared it. We are . . . things that the Others can use to amuse themselves. Maybe they can slip gently into the human mind and exercise their evil humor. Maybe they visit us from some far planet, a gaudy picnic for them, a stained excursion. And perhaps they laugh. . . .

THREE

RAUL KINSON'S WORLD HAD WALLS. IT WAS A WORLD of rooms, of ramps, of corridors.

There was nothing else. Thought could not reach *beyond* the walls, beyond the furthest rooms. He had tried to thrust his thoughts *through* the walls, but thoughts cannot encompass the idea of nothingness, and so his thoughts curled back, repelled by a concept beyond the authority of the mind.

When he was ten years old he had found the opening in the wall. It was an opening you could not crawl through, because it was covered with something you could look through as you look through water. Yet the substance was hard to the touch.

He was not yet old enough then to be permitted to dream.

Dreaming was for the older ones, the ones who had grown big enough to join the mating games.

In the ancient micro-books he had found the word for that hole in the wall. Window. He said it over and over. No one else read the micro-books. No one else knew the word. It was a secret that was precious, because it was not a made-up secret. It existed. Later, of course, he found that in the dreams there are many windows. They could be touched, opened, looked through. But not with one's *own* hands. That was the difference. In the dreams you had to use other hands, other bodies.

He would not forget the day he had found the window. The other children angered him. He had never liked the games they played. They laughed at him because he was not frail, as they were. His games, the muscle-stretching games, hurt them and made them cry out. On this day they had permitted him to play one of their games. The old game of statue dance, in one of the biggest rooms on the lowest level. One spindly girl held the two white blocks and as they danced the girl would unexpectedly clap the blocks together. At that signal everyone stopped as though turned to stone. But Raul had been off balance and when he tried to stop he crashed awkwardly into two of the frail boys, knocking them to the floor with shrill yelps of pain and pettish anger. They were angered but his anger surpassed theirs. The translucent floor glowed softly amber.

"You cannot play, Raul Kinson. You are rough. Go away, Raul. We won't let you play."

"I didn't want to play anyway. This game is silly."

He had left them and gone down the long hall that led through the maze of the power rooms where the air itself seemed to vibrate. He liked walking there as it gave him a strange but agreeable sensation in the pit of his stomach. Now, of course, he knew what the power rooms contained, and knew the name of the soft gray metal of the corridor walls in the power area. "Lead" it was called. Yet knowing what was in the power rooms had never decreased the pleasure he felt walking through the humming air, through a vibration below the range of audibility.

The day he walked away from their games he had wandered aimlessly. Memory was clear, though it had been fourteen years ago. He had been bored. The rooms where music played endlessly, had been playing since the beginning of time, and would play on forever, no longer pleased him. The grownups he saw ignored him, as was the custom.

Seeking some kind of excitement, he had stepped onto the moving track which carried him up through twenty levels to the place of the dreamers, where all children were forbidden to go. He had tiptoed down an empty silent corridor until he came to where the dreamers were, each in a thick glass case set into the wall.

He looked in at a woman. She lay on softness, curled, cat-slack, one hand under her cheek, the other touching her breast. Her mouth was distorted by the fitted metal plate between her teeth. Shining cables coiled up from the exposed edge of the plate and disappeared into the wall behind her shoulder. Standing close, he could feel a tiny throbbing, very much like that near the power rooms, but weaker.

As he watched her she suddenly stirred, and his sudden fright held him transfixed there as she took the plate from between her teeth, laid it aside, and reached down for her loose-woven robe of soft dull metal wadded near her feet, her movements slow and fumbling. As she began to yawn and to reach to push open the door of the glass case, she saw him and her slack sleepy face tightened at once in anger. He fled, knowing what the punishment would be, hoping that in the dimness she had not recognized him. He heard her call, sharp-voiced, "Boy! Stop!"

He ran as fast as he could, aware that if he took the track that moved slowly downward, her shouts might alarm someone on a lower level who could intercept him.

And so he dodged and ran up the stationary track that led to the twenty-first level. Once before he had explored up there. The silence of the rooms had awed him, had frightened him so that he had hurried back down, but on this day the silent rooms were refuge.

Higher and higher. The twenty-first level did not seem safe enough. He continued on up to the next level above that and collapsed, his mouth dry, a great pain in his side, his heart thudding. He listened above the sound of his heart and the stillness settled around him.

It was then he had noticed, close to his left hand, the edge of the great wheel that moved the track. It was like the wheels at the lower levels, with the one astounding difference—it was stilled.

Raul touched it gently. An odd new thought began to form itself in his mind. This might be a thing that was . . . broken. That had ceased to run. The thought dizzied him because it was outside his experience. All things ran —that is, all things designed to run did so, quietly, perfectly and forever. He had known of the tracks that were still above the twentieth level, and had thought that it was meant that they should be that way. And now he was confounded by this new concept of "brokenness." One of the women had broken an arm. She was shunned because it was now a crooked misshapen thing. He knew that he dared not talk of this new concept as it applied to the tracks above the twentieth level. Such a thought if expressed would be heresy, pure and simple.

It was hard to think in such a fashion. It made an ache deep in his head. If this track had ceased, for some reason, to run—then it followed that these upper levels were to be used by all the Watchers—and were shunned now merely because of the physical difficulty of walking up the steep slopes. He knew of no one, adult or child, who had gone higher than the twentieth level. There was no need for it. On the lower levels were the warm perfumed baths, the places of wine and of sleep and of the taste of honey. On the lower levels were the food rooms and the rooms that healed pain.

He suddenly wondered how high the levels stretched above him. Would it be possible to go to the top? But was there a top? Was there an end to it? Or did the levels go on and on, higher and higher, without ever an end to them. The strength of his desire for an answer to this question shocked him. He could taste the shrillness of fear in his throat, but at the same time excitement fluttered inside him with soft frantic wings.

He was dressed, as were all the children, in the single long strip of soft metal fabric. It was wound around the ~st. with the trailing end brought up between the legs and tucked firmly inside the waistband. When one was old enough to be permitted to dream, one was given either the toga and thongs of a man, or the robe of a woman. When death came, when the dead one was slipped, naked, into the mouth of the oval tube to speed down into unknown blackness, the clothing was saved. He had seen the room where it was stored in shining piles that reached to the highest point a man could touch.

He stood up, took a deep breath, tightened the hand at his waist and walked solemnly up the next motionless track. And the next, and the next. He tired of the steep climb and rested, realizing that he had lost count. The corridors down which he glanced had a sameness about them, and a silence.

At last he came to a track which moved upwards, its neighboring track moving downward, silently and perfectly. He stepped onto the track which carried him up, wondering how long it had been since other bare feet had stopped there.

Up and up and up. The familiar things were a frightening distance below him. But fears were lulled by the familiar silent motion of the track, which created a wind to touch his face.

With the sudden shock of a blow, he saw that at last there was no track to carry him higher, and thus no level above the one he had reached. The corridor was smaller than the others. He fought against a fear that commanded him to turn quickly and descend. The silence was the worst. No pad of feet against the body-warm floors. No distant voices. No sound of children. Just silence and the glow of the walls.

This, then, was the top of the world, the top of eternity, the summit of all. Fear faded into exaltation and he felt larger than life itself. He, Raul Kinson, had gone, alone, to the top of the world. The sneer at the others formed in his mind. He stuck his chest out and carried his chin high. The old ones said there was no limit to the world—that the silent levels went upward into infinity, that those who slid down the tube of death fell forever, turning slowly through the blackness, until the end of time.

He walked down the corridor. It curved slightly. He stopped. The was a picture, a large picture, at the end of the corridor. He knew of pictures. There were thousands of them on the eighteenth level and no one really understood them.

He walked to the picture with the contempt of familiarity. He walked close to its oddly shining surface. A low sound bubbled in his throat, the darkness rushed over him and he had no feeling of impact as he fell.

He struggled back to consciousness and knelt and looked at the picture again. He knew that it was no picture. It was a revelation. It was a truth so fantastic that he heard, on his lips, the meaningless sounds that infants make. He knew that from this day forward, he would be apart from all the others who had not seen this, who did not share his concept.

Outside of the levels, beyond the walls that glowed, everyone was taught that there was nothingness. Often he had gone to sleep trying to visualize "nothingness." It was all a lie.

All of the levels were located in an enormous, frightening room. The ceiling, impossibly high, was a deep purple color, with hard shining dots of light in it, and one enormous round deep-red light that hurt his eyes when he looked directly at it. The floor of the room was tan and brown and gray. The most horrible aspect of the enor-

mous room was his inability to see the walls. They were beyond vision, in itself a new concept. It dizzied him to stare down at the remote floor. Far off, to the right, the floor was humped up into a jagged series of mounds much higher than the level of his eye. And, in the foreground, six objects towered, standing neatly in a row. The glow of the round red light made them look silvery. The longer he stared, the more accustomed he became to perspective and the more accurately he could assess the height of those six cylindrical featureless objects with the blunt snouts and the flared portion that rested against the tan of the floor. As he watched he saw movement. A bit of the floor came alive, lifted up into a tall whirling column. He could not understand why it did this thing. He watched it move, still whirling, toward the high rough mounds. Soon he could see it no more. He touched his mouth to the hard surface of the transparent substance and drew back with startled speed. In a world where everything was warmed, the surface had a strange chill.

The gnawing of hunger at last took him away from the picture which he later found was called a "window." He went all the way back down to the deep familiar levels. He spoke to no one of what he had seen. He walked in a daze, feeling shrunken and small against the enormities of what lay outside the known world. He ate and slept and bathed and walked alone, seeking always the chance to slip away, to return to his window that looked out on another world which dwarfed his own.

Once, full of the importance of new knowledge, he had tried to tell one of the old ones about what he had seen. Wrath exploded and Raul Kinson picked himself up off the floor, with bleeding mouth, determined to speak no more.

With Leesa, of course, it was a different thing. As his sister, she shared, to some extent, that wry biological joke which had given him a deep chest, broad shoulders, strong column of neck, muscle-bulge of thigh and calf in a world where physical strength was useless.

He remembered that he had been twelve and she was

ten when he took her up to the window. At ten she was taller and stronger than the other girl children of the same age. Like Raul, her hair was blue-black and abundant. It set them apart in a world where hair was thin, dry and brown, lasting usually until the age of twenty, seldom beyond.

They had talked, and he knew that Leesa shared his vague feeling of disquiet, his aimless discontent—but her releases took a different form. Whereas he strove constantly to learn more, to understand more, she made a fetish of wildness and childish abandon.

He was proud of the way she refused to show her fear. They stood at the window. He said, proud of his new words, "That is 'outside.' All of our world and all the levels are inside of what is called a 'building.' It is cold out there. That red round light is a sun. It moves across the ceiling, but never goes completely out of sight. I have watched it. It travels in a circle."

Leesa looked at it calmly enough. "It is better inside."

"Of course. But it is a good thing to know—that there is an outside."

"Is it? Why is it good just to know things? I would say it is good to dance and sing and be warm—to take the long baths and find the foods that taste best."

"You won't tell anyone about this?"

"And be punished? I am not that stupid, Raul."

"Come, then. And I will show you other things."

He took her down several levels to a series of small rooms. He took her to one room where ten chairs faced the end of the room. He made her sit in one while he went to the machine which had taken him so many months to understand. He had broken four of them before he at last found the purpose.

Leesa gasped as the light dimmed and the pictures appeared, by magic, on the wall at the end of the room, the end that they faced.

Raul said quietly, "I believe it was intended that all children should be brought to these rooms to watch the images. But somehow, a long time ago, it was given up.

Those marks under each picture mean nothing to you, Leesa. But I have learned that they are writing. Each thing has a word, as you know. But those marks can mean the word. With those marks, if you could read, I could tell you something without talking."

"Why would you want to do that?" Her tone was full of wonder.

"I could leave a message for you. I can read the writing under the pictures. There is an uncountable number of these spools to put in the machines. Each room holds ones more complicated than in the previous room. I think that this room was for the very small children, because the words are simple."

"You are clever, Raul, to understand those marks. But it seems like a hard thing to do. And I don't know why you do it."

Her wonder had changed to boredom. He frowned. He wanted someone to share this new world with him.

He remembered a place that would interest her. He took her down several levels to a much larger room. This time the pictures moved and they seemed to have real dimensions and the persons, oddly dressed, talked, using strange words scattered among those more familiar.

Raul said, "That is a story. I can understand it because I have learned the strange words—at least some of them." In the dim light he saw her leaning forward, lips parted. The people in peculiar dress moved in strange rooms.

He turned it off. "Raul! It's . . . beautiful. Make it appear again."

"No. You don't understand it."

"It is like what I imagine the dreams must be, like they will be when we're old enough to be allowed to dream. And I thought I could never wait. Please, Raul. Show me how to make it happen again."

"No. You have no interest in these things. In women that wear strange colors and men that fight. Go on back down to your games, Leesa."

She tried to strike him and then she wept. Finally he

pretended to relent. "All right, Leesa. But you must start like I did. With the simple pictures. With the simple writing. And when you learn, then you can see all this again and you'll understand it."

"I'll learn today!"

"In a hundred days. If you are quick and if you spend many hours here."

He took her back to the first room and tried to help her. She wept again with frustration. At last the corridors dimmed and they knew that the time of sleep had come. Time had gone too quickly. They hurried back down to the others, hiding until the way was clear, then strolling in with exaggerated calm.

At sixteen Raul Kinson towered above every man in the world. He knew that it was time, and that the day was coming. He knew it from the way the women looked at him, from a new light in their eyes, a light that troubled him. They could not speak to him because until he was empowered to dream, he was still a child.

There were those who had certain duties. And, in each case, they instructed a young one of their choice in these duties in preparation for the time of death. There was a woman in charge of the rooms of childbirth, and another who cared for the young children. A man, fatter than others, organized the games of the adults. But of all those with special duties, Jord Orlan was the most powerful. He was aloof and quiet. He was in charge of dreams and the dreamers. He had wise, kind eyes and a face with a sadness of power in it.

Jord Orlan touched Raul Kinson lightly on the shoulder and led him to the far end of the tenth level, to the chambers where Jord Orlan lived alone, apart from the community life.

Raul felt a trembling excitement within him. He sat where Jord Orlan directed him to sit. He waited.

"After today, my son, you cease to be a child. All who are no longer children must dream. It is the privilege of being an adult. Those of you who come to me come with many wrong ideas of the dreams. That is because it is forbidden to discuss the dreams with children. Many of our people take the dreams too lightly. That is regrettable. They feel that the dreams are pure and undiluted pleasure, and they forget the primary responsibility of all those who dream. I do not wish you, my son, to ever forget that primary responsibility. In good time I shall explain it to you. In our dreams we are all-powerful. I shall take you to the glass case of dreams which shall be yours until the time of death. And I will show you how to operate the mechanism which controls the dreams. But first we shall talk of other matters. You have remained apart from the other children. Why?"

"I am different."

"In body, yes."

"And in mind. Their pleasures have never interested me."

Orlan looked beyond him. "When I was small, I was the same."

"May I ask questions? This is the first time I have been permitted to talk to an adult in this way."

"Of course, my son."

"Why are we called the Watchers?"

"I have been puzzled about that. I believe that it is because of the dreams. The source of the word is lost in antiquity. Possibly it is because of the fantastic creatures that we watch in our dreams."

"You say that those creatures are fantastic. They are men?"

"Of course."

"Which, then, is the reality? This constricted place or the open worlds of the dreams?" In his intense interest Raul had forgotten to use only the familiar words.

Jord Orlan looked at him sharply. "You have strange language, my son. Where did you obtain it? And who told you of the 'open worlds'?"

Raul stammered, "I . . . I made up the words. I guessed about open worlds."

"You must understand it is heresy to ever consider the

creatures of the dreams as reality. The machines for dreaming have a simple principle, I believe. You are familiar with the vague, cluttered dreams of childhood. The machines merely clarify and make logical these dreams through some application of power. They are limited in that there are only three areas, or worlds, in which we can dream. In time you will become familiar with each world. But never, never delude yourself by believing that these worlds exist. The only possible world is here, on these levels. It is the only conceivable sort of surroundings which will permit life to exist. We become wiser men through dreaming."

Raul hesitated. "How long has this world of ours existed?"

"Since the beginning of time."

"Who . . . who made it? Who built these walls and the dream machines?"

"Again, my son, you come close to heresy in your questions. All this has always existed. And man has always existed here. There is no beginning and no end."

"Has anyone ever thought that a larger world might exist outside the levels?"

"I must ask you to stop this questioning. This life is good and it is right for all of the nine hundreds of mankind. Nothing exists beyond the walls."

"May I ask just one more question?"

"Of course. Provided it has more sense than your previous questions."

"I have seen that this world is large, as though many more men once lived in it than do now. Are our numbers smaller than in times past?"

Orlan abruptly turned his back. His voice came softly to Raul's ears. "That question has bothered me. I have not thought of it for a long time. When I was very small there were over a thousand of us. I have wondered about this thing. Each year there are one or two togas or robes for which no children are born." His voice strengthened. "But it will be of no importance in our lifetime. And I cannot believe that man will dwindle and die out of the

world. I cannot believe that this world will one day be
empty when the last person lies dead with no one to as-
sist him into the tube."

Orlan took Raul's hand. "Come and I will take you to
the case assigned to you for all of your life."

Orlan did not speak until they stood, on the twentieth
level, before the empty case. Orlan said, "At your head,
as you lie therein, you will touch that small knurled knob.
It has three stations for the three dream worlds. The first
station is marked by a line which is straight. That is the
most beautiful world of all. The second station is marked
by a curved line which stands on a base. You will find
that world frightening at first. It is noisy. The third station, marked with a line with a double curve, is to direct
the machine to create the third world, the one we find of
least interest. You will be free to dream at any time you
desire. You will shut yourself inside, set the knob for
whichever world you desire, then disrobe and take the
metal plate between your teeth and bite down on it firmly.
The dream will come quickly. In your dream you will have
a new body and new, odd, pointless skills. I cannot instruct
you how to acquire change and mobility in the worlds of
dreams. That is something you must learn by doing. Everyone learns quickly, but the actual procedure does not
lend itself to words. You will dream for ten hours at a
time and at the end of that time the machine will awaken
you. Then it is best to wait for a new day before dreaming
again."

Raul could not resist the chance to say, "When the
lights are bright in the walls and floors, we call it day,
and when they are dim, we call it night. Is there any particular reason for that?"

Jord Orlan's hand slid quickly down from Raul's
naked shoulder. "You talk insanely. Why do we have
heads? Why are we called men? Day is day and night is
night."

"I had a childhood dream where we lived on the outside of a great globe and there was nothing over us but
space. The other globe, which we called the sun, circled

us, giving light and heat. Day was when it was overhead. Night was when it was on the opposite side of the globe."

Orlan gave him a queer look. "Indeed?" he said politely. "And men lived on all sides of this globe?" Raul nodded. Orlan said triumphantly, "The absurdity is apparent! Those on the underside would fall off!" His voice became husky. "I wish to warn you, my son. If you persist in absurdities and in heresies, you will be taken to a secret place that only I know of. It has been used in times past. There is a door and beyond it is an empty coldness. You will be thrust out of the world. Is that quite clear?"

Sobered, Raul nodded.

"And now you must dream of each world in turn. And at the end of three dreams you will return to me and you will be told the Law."

Jord Orlan walked away. Raul stood by the case, trembling. He lifted the glass door, slid quickly in and lay on his back on the softness.

He unwound the band of fabric and thrust it from him. The soft throb of power surrounded him, tingling against his naked limbs. He set the knob at figure 1, which Orlan had not known as a figure, as a mathematical symbol.

The metal plate was cool to his touch. He stretched his lips and put it between his teeth. Putting his head back he shut his teeth firmly against the metal . . . and fell down into the dream as though he fell from the great red sun to the brown dusty plains near the ragged mountains.

He fell remote and detached in the blackness, limbless, faceless. . . .

All motion stopped. This then, was the precious dream? Absolute nothingness, absolute blankness, with only the sense of existence. He waited and slowly there came to him an awareness of dimension and direction. He hung motionless, and then detected, at what felt like a great distance, another entity. He felt it was a sense that was not sight or touch or hearing. He could only think of it as an awareness. And with the power of his mind he thrust out toward it. The awareness heightened. He thrust again and again and it was a sudden merging. The thing he merged with fought him. He could feel it twist and try to turn away. He held it without hands, pulled it toward him without arms. He pulled it in and merged it with himself and pushed it back and down and away from him so that it was shrunken into a far small corner.

And Raul Kinson found himself walking on a dusty road. His arm hurt. He looked down at it and he was shocked to see the stringy leanness of the arm, the harsh metal enclosing the withered wrist, the dried blood where the metal had cut him. He was dressed in soft rags and he smelled the stink of his body. He limped on a bruised foot. The metal band on his wrist was in turn connected to a chain affixed to a long heavy pole. He was one of many men fastened to one side of the pole, with an equal number attached to the other side. Ahead of him, bare strong shoulders, oddly dark, were crisscrossed with wounds, some fresh, some very old.

The thing he held pressed down, writhed, and he released the pressure, a pure mental pressure he could not understand. It seemed to flow up into his mind, bringing with it strong fear and hate and the strange words of a strange tongue which, oddly, had meaning to him. These others were his comrades. Yes, they had fought together against the soldiers of Arrud the Elder, seven days' march away. Death was better than captivity. Now there was nothing to look forward to but an empty belly, a life of slavery and savage punishment, a ceaseless, hopeless desire to escape and return to the far green fields of Raeme, to the cottage where the woman would wait for a time, where the children played by the mud sill of the door.

Vision and other senses began to fade. Raul found that he had released the mind of this man too far, that he had given the man the power to thrust him back into the nothingness. So once again he exerted control. In a short time he found the necessary delicate balance—with the captured mind thrust down, but not so far that language and circumstances became meaningless, yet with a sufficient control so that his own will would not be thrust out.

With the maintenance of a proper balance, it was as though he existed on two levels. Through the mind of this man, this person who called himself Laron, he felt the hate and the hopeless anger, and also, through the alien invasion of his mind, a secondary fear of madness.

He trudged along in the dust. The soldiers guarding them carried long pikes with metal tips and walked lightly, joking among themselves, calling the prisoners foul names.

Raul gasped with pain as the pike point stabbed his upper arm. "Scrawny old one," the soldier said. "You'll be lion meat tomorrow, if you live that long."

Ahead the dusty road wound back and forth up the flank of a hill. Beyond the hill he could see the white towers of the city where Arrud the Elder ruled his kingdom with traditional ferocity. It appeared to be a march of many hours. What had Jord Orlan said about change and mobility? A knack to be acquired. This helplessness and the pain of walking did not seem to promise much.

He let the captive mind flow back up through secret channels, once again taking over will and volition. Senses faded, and as the nothingness once again enfolded him, he tried to thrust out toward the side, toward the soldiers. Again the feeling of grappling with a strange thing that resisted. The moment of control, of pushing the other entity down into a corner of his mind passed and vision returned.

He lay on his belly in a patch of brush, staring down at a distant dusty road far below, at a clot of figures walking slowly along the road. He let the captive mind expand until he could feel its thoughts and emotions. Once again —hate and fear. This one had escaped from the city. He was huge and strong. He carried a stout club and he had killed three men in making his escape. Contempt and pity for the captives. Hate for their captors. Fear of discovery. This was a simpler, more brutal mind than the first one. Easier to control. He watched for a time, then slid out of the mind and thrust his way toward the remembered direction of the road.

The new entity was more elusive and control more difficult. He found that he had taken over the body of a young soldier. He walked apart from the others. The captives were at his right, laboring under the weight of the poles that kept them joined, like one large many-legged insect. Raul fingered the spirit of this young soldier and found there revulsion for the task, contempt for the calloused sensibilities of his comrades in arms, pity for the dirty prisoners. He regretted the choice of occupation he had made and wished with all his heart that this duty was over. It would be better in the city at dusk when he could wander among the bazaars, a soldier returned from the wars, stopping at the booths to buy the spiced foods he loved.

Raul forced a turn of the head and looked back at the line. After several moments he found the thin man with the pike wound in his upper arm. He had been in that man's mind. Inside his own mind he felt the flutter of panic of the young soldier who had made a motion without apparent purpose. "Why do I turn and stare at the thin old one? Why is he of more importance than the others? Is the sun too hot on this helmet?"

Raul turned and looked up into the hills, trying to locate the brush where the fugitive hid. This seemed to alarm the captive mind even more.

"Why am I acting so strangely?"

The haft of the pike was comforting in Raul's hand. He lifted it a trifle, realizing that the habit action patterns of the young soldier would serve him well should he wish to use the pike. For a time he contented himself with looking about at the landscape, picking out of the soldier's mind the names of the objects he saw. A bird, a quick blue flash against the sky. An ox cart loaded with husks of corn. They passed stone ruins of an unguessed antiquity.

He turned when he heard a harsh scream. The thin one, whose mind he had inhabited, had fallen. A heavyset soldier, his face angry and shiny with sweat, jabbed again and again with the pike, making the red blood flow.

Raul thrust with the ease of long practice, the tip of
pike tearing through the profiled throat of the heav
soldier, who turned, eyes bulging. He clawed at his th
with both hands, dropped to his knees, then toppled
down into the yellow dust of the road.

In his mind he felt the panicky thoughts of the yo
soldier. "I killed him! I must be mad! Now I'll be kill

The soldier in charge swaggered over, scowling
took in the situation at a glance and drew the s
broadsword that only he wore. The others, grinnin
anticipation, kept the young soldier from fleeing by
ing a half-circle of leveled pikes.

Raul, infected by the panic in his mind, thrust
with the pike. The broadsword flickered and lopped
two-foot section of the end of the pike, stinging his h
He looked down and saw the thrust as the broads
went deep into his belly. The leader twisted the blad
withdrew it. The spasm and cramp dropped Raul t
hands and knees. He gagged as his arms weakene
his face sank slowly toward the dust. From the corn
his eye he saw the broadsword flash up again. The
pain across the back of his neck drove him out int
nothingness where there was neither sight, nor soun
sense of touch.

At dusk he was in the city, with life and motion
ing and clashing around him. He lead a heavily
burro and at intervals he cried out that he had
cool water for dry throats. In the mind of the wate
dor he found the location of the palace itself. Mo
more he was gaining control of the directional t
gaining confidence in gauging the distance from
mind. He was a guard at the castle gates, then a ma
carried a heavy load up endless stone steps.

At last he became Arrud the Elder, the man of
To his astonishment, as he gained control of the
mind, he found it as simple and brutal as the min
fugitive. He found hate and fear there. Hate of the
kings who drained his manpower and wealth in u

wars. Fear of treachery within the palace walls. Fear of assassination.

Raul relaxed to Arrud's action patterns. Arrud buckled the heavy belt around his thick waist. It was of soft leather, studded with bits of precious metal. He flung the cape over his wide shoulders, tucked his thumbs under the belt and swaggered down the stone hallway, thrusting open the door at the end of the corridor. The woman had long hair, the color of flame. She lay back on the divan and looked at Raul-Arrud coldly. She had a harsh, cruel mouth.

"I await your pleasure," she said bitterly.

"Tonight we look at the prisoners. The first ones have arrived."

"This time, Arrud, pick some strong ones for the beasts, strong ones who will fight and make the game last."

"We need the strong ones for work on the walls," he said sulkily.

Her tone grew wheedling. "Please. For me, Arrud. For Nara."

Raul relinquished his hold and faded into grayness. Only the gentlest of motions was necessary. He seeped slowly and relentlessly into the mind of the woman and found that there was an elusive subtlety about it that defied his initial attempts at control. At last he had her mind trapped. Her thoughts were hard to filter through his own mind. They were fragmentary, full of flashes of brilliance and color. Only her contempt and hate for Arrud was constant, unvarying. He found that maintaining a delicate balance of control was far more difficult when handling the woman-mind. He would possess her mind so utterly that he would lose her language, her female identity, to become, foolishly, Raul in a woman-body. Then she would surge back until he clung to the last edge of control.

In a short time he knew her. Knew Nara, daughter of a foot soldier, dancer, mistress of a captain, and then a general, and at last mistress of Arrud. He knew her contemptuous acknowledgment of the power of hair like flame, body that was cat-sleek, vibrant, clever.

Arrud came near the divan. He pressed his knuckles to his forehead, said slowly, "For a time I felt odd, in my mind. As though a stranger were in my mind, calling me from a great distance."

"You have not given me your promise about the strong slaves, Arrud."

He looked down at her. He reached with a hard hand, fondled her breast, hurting her with his clumsiness. She pushed his hand away and his lips went tight. He reached again, tore the sheer fabric of her garment from throat to thigh.

Raul fingered through her thoughts and memories, found the knowledge of the ivory-hilted dagger wedged between the cushions of the divan. He forced the woman's mind back, quelling her anger, supplanting it with fear. She willed herself to speak and he would not permit her to speak. Arrud slid with bulky clumsiness onto the couch, seeking the woman's throat with his lips. Raul forced the woman's hand to grasp the dagger. She was rigid with fear and he sensed in her mind the frantic thought that this was not the way to kill Arrud. This way she would be discovered. The dagger tip touched Arrud's back. The needle blade slid into the thick muscles as though sliding through water as it reached for the heart. His heavy body pinned her to the couch as he died. As Raul slid away, sickened and weary, he heard her first maddened scream.

Raul awakened in the glass case of dreams. He lay still for a time, and there was a deep, slow, aimless lethargy within him, an exhaustion more of the spirit than of the mind or body. The ten-hour dream had ended as he left the body of the woman. It seemed as though he had been in the odd, alien world for months. He took the metal plate from his mouth. His jaw muscles were cramped and sore. He turned slowly and pushed the side panel up, turned and rested bare feet on the warm floor of the level of dreams.

A woman stood there, smiling at him. The habits of childhood were difficult to overcome. It shocked him that he should be noticed by one of the adult women. She was not an old one.

"You have dreamed," she said.

"A long dream and it tired me."

"The dreams are like that in the beginning. I shall never forget my first dream. You are Raul. Do you know my name?"

"I remember you from the games of the children. A long time ago you became a dreamer. Fedra, is it not?"

She smiled at him. "I am glad you remembered." It was flattering to be treated with such friendliness by an adult. Childhood was a lonely time. Fedra was different, in the same way that he and Leesa were different, but not as much. She merely had not quite the frailness of the others, and there was some lustre to her brown hair.

He reached for his garment in the case, but she said, "Have you forgotten?"

He looked at her. She held the toga of a man in one hand, the thongs in the other. His heart gave a leap. To think of all the times he had yearned for a man's toga. And now it was here. His. He reached for it. She pulled it back.

"Do you not know the custom, Raul? Were you not told?"

Her tone was teasing. He remembered then. The man's toga and thongs must be put on the first time by the woman who will partner the man in the first mating dance he is privileged to attend. He paused in confusion.

She drew back and her mouth became unpleasant. "Maybe you think, Raul Kinson, that you would prefer another. It will not be easy for you. You are not liked. Only two of us asked, and the other changed her mind before the drawing."

"Give those to me," he said, his anger matching hers.

She backed away. "It is not permitted. It is the law. If you refuse, you must wear child's clothing."

He stared at her and thought of Nara with the hair like flame, the dusky body. Compared to Nara this woman was mealy-white, soft. And he saw the unexpected sheen of tears in her eyes, tears that came from the hurt to her pride.

So he stood and closed the panel on his case of dreams and permitted her to drape the toga on his shoulders, fasten the belt, with the slow stylized motions of the custom. She knelt and wound a silver thong around his right ankle, bringing the two ends of the thong around his leg in opposite directions, each turn higher so that the thong made a diamond pattern. She knotted it firmly with the traditional knot just below his knee. He advanced his left leg and she placed the thong on it. She still knelt, staring up at him. He remembered, reached and took her hands, pulled her to her feet.

Together, with not another word, they rode down from the higher levels to the proper corridor. They went back to the room where the others waited. The fat old one who directed the games of the adults glanced at them with relief. He went to the music panel and touched the soft red disc which started the music. The other couples ceased chattering and lined up. Raul felt like a child who had stolen the toga and thongs of a man. His hands trembled and his knees felt weak as he took his place in line, facing Fedra. He watched the other men from the corner of his eye.

The fat old one played a sustained note on the silver tube he wore around his neck. Naked skulls gleamed in the amber glow of the walls. The cold, formal, intricate dance, substitute for urge and need, began. Raul felt that he moved in a dream. The quick harsh world he had visited seemed more to his taste than this stylized substitution. He sensed the amusement in the others, knew that they saw the awkwardness of his hands and feet, knew that this same awkwardness shamed Fedra. This dance was required, he knew, because it meant continuance of the world of the Watchers.

As the music slowly increased in tempo, Raul wished that he were hiding on one of the highest levels. He forced himself to smile like the others.

FOUR

BARD LANE STOOD AT THE WINDOW OF HIS OFFICE STAR-ing out across the compound toward a new barracks building that was being constructed between two older ones. The wire mesh had been stretched taut and a crew with spray guns were spreading the plastic on the wire with slow practised strokes.

General Sachson had not underestimated the pressure. It was coming from all directions. A Cal Tech group had published an alleged refutation of the Beatty Theories, and the news services had picked it up, simplified it. *Credo,* the new micro-magazine, was screaming about "billions being squandered in some crackpot experimentation in the mountains of northern New Mexico."

A group of lame-duck congressmen was sublimating political frustration by taking a publicity-conscious hack at the top-heavy appropriations for space conquest. A spokesman for the JCS hinted at a complete reorganization of the top management of military-civilian space flight efforts.

Sensing the possibility of cancellation of Project Tempo, the administrative branches in Washington—finance, personnel, procurement—were pulling the reins tight by compounding the numbers of reports necessary.

Sharan Inly tapped at the door and came into Bard's office. He turned and gave her a weary smile. She wore her usual project costume, jeans and a man's white shirt with the sleeves rolled high, collar open.

She glanced with distaste at the mound of paper on his desk. "Bard, are you a clerk or a scientist?"

"I'm too busy learning to be the first to do anything about the second. I am beginning to learn something about government paper work, though. You know, I used to try to handle every report—at least set up reasonable procedure for it. Then I found out that before I can get a report in, the whole thing is changed around. Know what I do now?"

"Something drastic?"

"I had rubber stamps made. Take a look. See this one? HOLD FOR ACTION—COORDINATION GROUP. And this one. FOR REVIEW AND REPORT—STATISTICAL COMMITTEE. Here is a pretty one. SUSPENSE FILER—PROGRAMMING BOARD."

"What on earth are they for?"

"Oh, it's very simple. Now take this report request right here. See, it came in three copies. The Industrial Research Committee of the Planning Board of the Materials Allocation Group of the Defense Control Board wants a report. And I quote. 'It is requested that on the twelfth and twenty-seventh of each month, beginning with the month following receipt of this directive, that the planned utilization of the appended list of critical metals be reported for three months in the future, each month's utilization to be expressed as a percentage of total utilization during the six months period immediately preceeding each report.' And here is their appended list. Seventeen items. Did you see that new girl in my outer office, in the far corner?"

"The little brunette? Yes, I saw her."

"Well, I route this report to her. She cuts a stencil and mimeographs the directive, runs off a hundred copies. She's my Coordination Group, my Statistical Committee and my Programming Board. On the twelfth and twenty-seventh of each month she'll mail in a copy of the directive with one of the rubber stamp marks on it. She'll send one to the Defense Control Board and one to the Materials Allocation Group and one to the Planning Board and one to the Industrial Research Committee. I let her use any stamp she happens to feel like using at the moment. It seems to work just as well as making out the report. Probably better. I have her put a mysterious file number on the stencil."

"Oh, Bard, how terrible that your time has to be taken up with this sort of thing!"

"I don't mind most of them. But here's a rough one. No more personnel, Sharan. At least, they're making it so complicated to put on any new person that the delay will run into months. We'll have to make do with what we have. They're hamstringing me, very neatly. And I can't fight back. There's no one to fight. Just a big vague monster with carbon-paper tentacles, paper-clip teeth, and a hide made of layers of second sheets."

"Why, Bard? Why are they turning against the Project? They believed in it once."

"It's taking too long, I guess."

"Can't you go to Washington?"

"I'm no good at that sort of thing. I get a compulsion. I know what to say, how to butter them, but I can't quite manage to do it."

She went over to a heavy oak armchair near the window, dropped into it, hooked one slim leg over the arm. She frowned. He walked over and looked out the window, following her glance. "Well, Sharan, even if it never gets off the ground, they can't say that we didn't build a big one."

Even in the brightest sunshine, the light that shone down on the project area was diffused. Four gigantic steel towers of irregular size had been constructed in the form of an irregular oblong. A square mile of tough fabric, painted with all the art of camouflage, was suspended like a grotesque circus tent over the towers. From the air it would appear to be another barren irregular hill of rock and sage and sand. Bard Lane's office was near the cave-like lip of the south edge of the outsized tent. The Beatty

One stood in the middle of the tent. Around the base of the Beatty One was the constant, ant-like activity that had been going on for over a year.

Some of the labs were set into the solid rock of the surrounding hills. All project buildings not under the protection of the vast tent were designed to look, from the air, like just another sleepy village in the Sangre de Cristo Mountains, a village where the flagellationists still whip-cut the back of the selected man who labored under the heavy cross at Easter time.

He looked down at her for a moment, and resisted the impulse to rest his hand on her crisp hair, to feel, under his strong fingers, the delicate configuration of skull, the clean bone-line.

Bard locked his hands behind him and looked out to where he could see the dull metal base of the Beatty One, almost exactly one hundred and seventy feet in diameter, and so tall the round snout almost touched the fabric of the enormous tent. A platform elevator inched upward, carrying men in work clothes. The elevator was built on heavy steel circular tracks so that the operator could raise it to any point on the outside skin of the great vehicle.

"Does anybody expect it to fly, Doc?" she asked.

"I personally guarantee to get it at least twelve inches off the ground."

She smiled up at him, the smile flavored with rue. "News good and bad," she said. "The good is about Bill Kornal. We took him apart, every reflex, every neurosis, every response to stimuli, and we reassembled him. There is a change, sure. But it measures out as exactly as much as one would expect as an aftereffect of what happened to him. He is as sound and solid as that mountain over there."

"Good. Put him on. I'll sign the confirmation in the morning."

"And the bad news is that I can't find any real good reason to wash out Major Tommy Leeber. I don't have to like him, but I can't wash him out. Once you dig down through a lot of apparent complexities, the whole thing becomes very simple. He has a mind like a brass hinge. It works in just one direction: What is the best thing for Tommy Leeber? Totally directional, and of course he has a top security rating. So he's all yours, Bard. I brought him over. He's waiting out there for the deluxe tour."

Bard Lane glanced at his watch. "There's time. See you at dinner. Thanks for all the nice things you do for me."

Major Leeber had the same reaction as did every other newcomer to the project when he was finally taken close enough to the Beatty One to really appreciate the size of it. After he had been walked all the way around it, he finally shook himself out of his stunned air of disbelief, smiled his lazy smile and said, "So . . . I *still* don't believe it."

Dr. Bard Lane had the elevator brought to ground level and signaled the operator to take it up to the nose. He stood and leaned against a stanchion and watched Leeber move to the exact center of the platform. At the ogive curve, close under the overhead camouflage, the elevator tipped toward the hull and followed the curve on up to the last port. Leeber did not look well as he leaned away from the direction of the tilt.

"Come along," Bard said as he stepped over the lip of the port. He lowered himself to the deck inside, and began his familiar indoctrination speech as he gave the major a hand. "This will be the entrance port for the crew. The ship is designed for a crew of six. No passengers. The forward tenth of the overall length contains the living quarters, life maintenance systems, supplies and main control panels. We are in the control room. The three chairs there are on gymbals mounted on hydraulic pedestals designed to compensate for sudden increments in acceleration. They are similar to, but an improvement over, the systems previously used. Impulse screen mounted, as you can see, but not yet tied into either manual or computer control."

Leeber studied the main control panel and said,

"Looks like a king size A-six, and not too much different from the A-five. Where are the directional jets?"

"Eliminated in favor of a twenty-ton gyro that can be turned through a ten-degree arc. In free space it will turn her in any desired attitude. A lot of weight to boost, but not much less than standard attitude jet installation and the necessary fuel controls, and we save a lot by eliminating the initial lift-off with chemical fuels, so we have no booster stages to jettison on the way out."

"Initial lift on atomic drive? Poison the air?"

"With a very short-life emission. Launch site will be clean in ten hours. At half-diameter outbound, they switch to standard A fuel, and keep it on CA. That means that——"

"——at twelve thousand miles out they go right onto the same old A-six atomic propulsion fuel and stay in constant acceleration. I'm not a civilian, Doctor. So this marvelous ship is just one big son of a bitch of an oversized A-six with a flywheel gyro, a short-life mix for takeoff. Wonderful!" His smile was ironic, his eyes cold.

"With one more little change, Major. Eighty days of CA will put her clear of the system. Then they switch to Beatty Drive. Drive is an inaccurate word, but we haven't come up with a better one yet. I worked with Beatty and ran the team that completed his equations after he died two years ago. Do you have any background in theoretical physics?"

"Some exposure. Try me, Doctor."

"What does 'frames of reference' mean to you?"

"The old analogy about three elevators and one man in each one. Elevator A is going up at top speed, Elevator B is going down slowly and Elevator C is stuck between floors. Each one is moving at a different speed in relation to each of the other two."

"Very good. But you have one motionless elevator. Take it a step further. Your motionless one is at zero velocity. Okay, where is the motionless point in space? You can be hanging in space absolutely motionless in relation to one star, but moving at ten thousand miles per second

in relation to a star in some other direction. On a theoretical basis you would find a motionless point in space by
computing the velocity and direction of movement of all
the stars in all the galaxies and finding that point from
which all those velocities both toward you and away from
you, on whatever angle of inclination or declination,
would average out to zero. If we had the math to solve a
problem with an infinite number of unknowns, we do not
have all the knowns to feed into it, due to the temporal
limits—and physical limits—of observation. Are you with
it?"

"I think I . . . Well, keep going."

"Here is the heart of it. Beatty called that the space-
frame—the problem of finding the zero point in space. So
he made the assumption there must also be a time-frame.
He pictured a universe curved in upon itself in the
Einsteinian concept, but composed of not only varying velocities and directions, but also varying temporal relationships. From this he extrapolated the idea that an average
of the time relationships would give you a zero place, a
place where time does not exist, just as an average of
speed-relationships would give you a zero place where
movement does not exist. So he applied that theory to the
paradox of the expanding universe, and his equations did
what the red shift 'tired light' theories failed to do. He
proved that the apparent expansion was in fact the inter-
relationship of the velocity of light with a varying time
warp throughout the observable galaxies, with the effect
more apparent the greater the warp—i.e., in the most distant galaxies. I think I've lost you."

"Afraid so."

"Try it this way then. Until Beatty's work we believed
that maximum attainable velocity would always be a fractional percentage point under the speed of light itself, because according to the Fitzgerald equations, at the speed
of light the contraction of mass is infinite. Beatty gave us
a way to bypass that barrier by thrusting a ship into another frame of reference of time. Here is our standard
simplistic analogy. You are driving from El Paso to New

York. It will take you three days. You leave on Monday. You expect to get to New York on Wednesday. So as soon as you are outside the El Paso city limits you push a little button on the dashboard labeled 'Wednesday.' And there is the skyline of New York, right down the road."

"Didn't . . . the Fitzgerald equations say that time contracts along with mass in ratio to velocity?"

"Excellent, Major! Beatty's equations showed that the time gradient between different systems, instead of having to be traversed at nearly light speed, can be capsuled into an abrupt time shift, just as when you drive across from one time zone into the next."

"Your jumps would be a little bigger than Monday to Wednesday, I'd imagine."

"The increments are in standard segments of one hundred years. But don't think of it as a hundred years passing in a flash. It is more a distance measurement. You arrive in New York at the precise moment that you left El Paso."

"So when do you know when to make the jump, how far you'll jump, and where you'll be when you get there?"

Bard Lane shrugged and smiled. "That's what took seven months of programming and three months of integral and digital computer time. Then we built the control panels according to the results of the calculations."

"And that nut smashed them?"

"Do you mean Doctor Kornal? He did. He is back on the job. My decision to take him back will stand up, so don't step over the line you seem to be edging too close to."

"Me? Hell, let's be friends. Life is too short. It's your risk, not mine. What do we look at next?"

"Dinner. I'll take you through the labs tomorrow morning."

"Where do I find the action?"

"I'll point out the club on our way back down to the launch pad."

FIVE

BARD LANE SAT ON THE EDGE OF HIS BED. IT WAS after midnight on the same day that he had taken Major Leeber on the tour of inspection.

He sat and little rivulets of fear ran through his mind the way that rain will trickle erratically down a window-pane. The night was cool and the wind that came through the screen touched his naked chest and shoulders, but it did not stop the perspiration that made an oiled sheen on his face.

It was like a return to childhood, to the long-dead nights of terror. The scream. "Mommy, Mommy! It was a moldy man and he was sitting on my bed!"

"It's all right. It was just a dream, dear."

"He was here! He was! I saw him, Mommy."

"Shh, you'll wake your father. I'll sit here and hold your hand until you get back to sleep."

Sleep voice. "Well he *was* here."

He shivered violently. Now there was no one to call. There was someone you *should* call, but that might mean . . . defeat.

You can fight all the outside enemies in the world, but what if the enemy is in your own mind? What then?

It was a decision to make. He made it. He dressed quickly, snatched a leather jacket from the closet hook, shouldered his way into it as he left his quarters. From the slope he looked down on the project buildings. A thin moon rode high, silvering the dark buildings. He knew that inside the darkness there were lights, hum of activity, night shifts in the labs in the caves.

Sharan Inly had a room in the women's barracks. He walked down the slope and across the street. The girl at the switchboard was reading a magazine. She glanced up and smiled, "Good evening, Dr. Lane."

"Good evening. Dr. Inly, please. Would you connect the call in the booth?"

He shut himself in. Her voice was sleepy. "Hello, Bard."

"Did I wake you up?"

"Ten seconds later and you would have. What is it, Bard?"

He glanced through the booth door. The girl had returned to her magazine. "Sharan, would you please get dressed and come down. I must talk to you."

"You sound . . . upset, Bard. I'll be down in five minutes."

She was better than her word. He was grateful for her promptness. She came out beside him, asking no questions, letting him choose time and place. He led her over to the porch of the club. It was after hours and the chairs had been stacked on the tables. He set two of them on their legs. A dog howled in the hills. Over near the labor barracks someone laughed loudly.

"I want to consult you as a patient, Sharan."

"Of course. Who are you worried about?"

"Me."

"That sounds . . . absurd. Go ahead."

He made his voice flat, emotionless. "Tonight I had dinner with Major Leeber. I went back to my office to finish up some of the paperwork. It took a bit longer than I expected. When I finished, I was tired. I turned out the light and sat there in the dark for a few moments, waiting for enough energy to get up and go back to my quarters. I turned my chair and looked out the window. Enough moonlight came through the screen so that I could just make out the shape of the Beatty One.

"Suddenly, and without any warning, I felt a . . . nudge at my mind. That's the only way I can describe it. A nudge, and then a faint, persistent pushing. I tried to resist it, but its strength increased. There was a certain horrid

. . . confidence about it. An utterly alien pressure, Sharan. A calm pressure. Have you ever fainted?"

"Yes."

"Do you remember the way you tried to fight off the blackness, and it seemed to grow stronger? It was like that. I sat absolutely still, and even as I fought against it, one part of my mind was trying to find a reason for it. Tension, overwork, fear of failure. I used every device I could think of. I tried to focus my mind on nothing except the look of the corner of the screen. I dug my fingers into the chair arm and tried to focus on the pain. The thing in my mind increased the pressure and I had the feeling that it was *fitting* itself to my mind, turning as it entered, so as to find the easiest means of entrance. I lost the ability to control my own body. I could no longer dig at the chair arm with my fingers. I cannot describe how frightening that was. I have always felt . . . completely in control of myself, Sharan. Maybe I've been too confident. Possibly even contemptuous of the aberrations of others.

"My eyes were still focused at short range on the corner of the screen. My head lifted a bit and, without willing it, found myself staring out at the Beatty One, trying to make out outlines. It was in my mind, strongly, that I was seeing the ship for the first time. I was sensing the reaction of the thing that had entered my mind. The thing was perplexed, awed, wondrous. Sharan, in that state, I could have been forced to do . . . anything. Destroy the ship. Kill myself. My will and my desires would have had no part in action I might have undertaken."

As she touched his arm, and said softly, "Easy, mister," he realized that his voice had climbed into a higher register, threatening shrillness.

He took a deep breath. "Tell me, is there such a thing as a waking nightmare?"

"There are delusions, fantasies of the mind."

"I felt . . . possessed. There, I've said it. The thing in my mind seemed to be trying to tell me that it was not inimical, that it wished no harm. When the pressure reached its strongest point, the moonlight faded away. I looked into blackness and I felt that all my thoughts and memories were being . . . handled. Fingered, picked at.

"And now, Sharan, comes the part that's pure nightmare. The thing pressed its own thought images into my mind. It was as though it substituted its memories for mine. I looked down a long, wide corridor. The floors and walls had a muted glow. The people had an almost sexless look, frail, neuter, blue-white people, but human. It was very clear they were inbred. They walked with a tired timelessness, a semi-hypnotic sort of dedication, as though every movement was a portion of custom rather than habit. And suddenly I was looking out through a hug window, a window at an enormous distance from ground level. Six cigar-shaped, tail-finned objects that could only have been space ships pointed upward at a purple sky and a huge dying red sun that filled a quarter of the sky. I realized that I was seeing a dying world, an ancient world, and the people who were left in it. I got an impression of sadness, of a remote and weary sadness. Then the presence flicked out of my mind so quickly that it dizzied me. My own will, which seemed to have been crowded back into a tiny corner of my brain, re-expanded suddenly and I was myself again. I tried to treat it as a . . . as something of no importance. I went back to my quarters and undressed, as though I could go to bed with no further thought of it. But I had to come and tell you about this."

He waited. Sharan stood up, walked to a post set into the cement porch, leaned against it with her hands in her pockets, her back to him.

"Bard," she said, "we talked about the X factor in mental illness. In psychiatry we have a recurrent phenomenon. A mind, temporarily out of focus, will use as material for delusion something that has happened in the immediate past. Our sleeping dreams, as you know, are almost always based on some reference to the previous waking period. Recently we have talked of being possessed by devils. Silly darn phrase. Bill told us his symptoms. What is more natural than for you to borrow his symptoms and use them as your own. But, of course, you carried it a step further, due

to your background and your ambition. You had to make
the devils into representatives of some extra-solar super-
race, because you are too practical to be satisfied with an
illusion of devils. Bard, this is all due to the pressure
mounting, the fear that they'll stop the project, the nee-
dling General Sachson gave you." She turned and faced
him, hands still in the pockets of the jeans.

"Bard, go on back to bed. We'll stop at my place and
I'll bring you down a little pink pill."

"I haven't made you understand, have I?"

"I think I understand."

"Dr. Inly, tomorrow I'll report to you for the usual
tests. You will advise me if you find anything out of line. If
so, I shall make my resignation effective at once."

"Don't be a child, Bard! Who else could carry Project
Tempo on his back? Who else could get the loyalty yo·· ¹¹
out of fifteen hundred of us working out here in this Goa-
forsaken spot on something not one in fifty of us can understand?"

"Suppose," he said harshly, "that the next time I have
this little aberration, I get as destructive as Kornal did?"

She walked slowly to him, pulled her chair closer, sat
down and took his left hand in both of hers. "You won't,
Bard."

"I believe it's part of your job to be reassuring, isn't it?"

"And to wash out those who show signs of incipient
mental instability. Don't forget that. Part of my job is to
watch you. I have been watching you. I have a complete
file on you, Bard. For one moment, look at yourself objec-
tively. Thirty-four years old. Born in a small town in Ohio.
Orphaned at eight. Raised by an uncle. Public school. At
twelve you had your own ideas of the way to solve the
problems in the geometry book. You were skeptical of the
Euclidian solutions. You won a science scholarship based
on the originality of an experiment you did in the high
school physics lab. You worked for the other money you
needed. Cal Tech, M.I.T. You got a reputation when you
helped design the first practical application of atomic
power for industrial use. Government service. Years of ex-

hausting labor on the A-four, A-five and A-six. Now do you know why you had this little . . . lapse in your office?"

"What do you mean?"

"You have no ability to relax. You've never had time for a girl, for a lost weekend. You've never fallen asleep under a tree, or caught a trout. When you read for amusement, you read scientific papers and new texts. Your idea of a happy evening is either to cover fifteen pages of blank paper with little Greek chicken-tracks, or have a bull session with some men who are just as one-sided as you are."

"Does the doctor want to prescribe?" he asked gently.

She snatched her hand away and leaned back in the chair. The moon had slanted low enough so that under the porch overhang it touched the line of her cheek, made a faint highlight on her lower lip, left her eyes shadowed.

After a long silence she said, "The doctor will prescribe the doctor, Bard. I'll come back to your quarters with you, if . . . you'll have me."

He was aware of his own intense excitement. He let the seconds go by. He said, "I think we'd better be thoroughly honest with each other, Sharan. It's the best way. You've put us into a delicate spot. Emotions are pretty well exposed at this point. I know your personal loyalty to me, and to the project. I know your capacity for loyalty. Now answer this honestly, my dear. If I had not come to you with this . . . trouble, would you have made that sort of offer?"

"No," she whispered.

"And if I had asked you, in the casual way that seems to have become a custom these past few years?"

"I don't know. Probably no, Bard. I'm sorry."

"Then let's drop the subject, with no harm done. I'll settle for a pink pill and an appointment in the morning."

"And after you are tested, Bard, I am going to send you out into the hills with a scope rifle I can borrow from a friend of mine. You are going to spend a full day potting varmints and thinking of something beside this damnable project. That's an order."

"Yes, *sir!*" he said, standing up and saluting.

"Please, Bard. You must understand that it was just weakness which made you feel that you had the symptoms Bill Kornal described. A weakness born of tension and strain. It was auto-hypnosis, pure and simple. It can happen to any of us."

"Whatever it was, Sharan, I didn't like it. Come on. I'll walk you back."

They went slowly down the road. There was no need for conversation between them. She had partially comforted him. After he was in bed, waiting for the mild drug to take effect, he wondered why he had been so reluctant to permit her to sacrifice her own integrity for the sake of the project. He thought of the slim clean look of her in the moonlight, of her young breasts against the fabric of her jacket. He smiled at his own reservations, at his reluctance to accept such a gift. They had both sensed that they were almost—but not quite—right for each other. And "not quite" was not enough for either of them.

SIX

RAUL KINSON REALIZED THAT EIGHT YEARS HAD PROVED Fedra correct. One never forgets those first few dreams, those first three dreams—one for each alien world demarked on the dial at the head of the dream case.

Fedra had borne his child during that first year of the dreams. Sometimes he watched the children at their games, and wondered which one was his. He looked in vain for any sign of resemblance. He wondered at this curiosity, which the others did not seem to share.

Yes, the first dreams could never be forgotten. Even after eight years he remembered every moment of the second dream.

In his second dream he had a new certainty of contact,

a new assurance born of the practice during the first dream. He was eager to see this second world. In his initial eagerness he had grasped the first contact mind, had thrust with all the power of intellect, motivated by strong curiosity.

And at once he had found himself in an alien body which writhed in bright hot light on a hard surface. He could not control the muscles or the senses of the captive body. Vision was broken fragments. Muscle spasms could not be controlled. He tried to withdraw pressure, but the host mind would not take over the body again. The brain he touched was shattered, irrational, sending messages of spasm to uncontrolled muscles. At first he thought he had inhabited a mind already broken, and then he began to guess that perhaps the full, uncontrolled thrust of his own mind had broken the host mind. He gave up all efforts at control and slid out of the host, impelling himself very gently toward the nearest contact.

He slid with restraint into this new mind, never taking over control, merely waiting and watching and listening at a sufficiently high level so that the language became clear. The new host was a brawny man in a blue uniform. He was saying, "Move back there! You! Give the guy air! Give him a chance, folks."

A second man in uniform came over. "What you got, Al?"

"Fella with a fit or something. I sent in an ambulance call. You there, did I hear you say you're a doctor? Take a look at him, will you?"

A man in gray bent over and wedged a pencil between the teeth of the man who writhed on the sidewalk. He looked up at the policeman. "Epileptic, I think. Better send for an ambulance."

"Thanks, Doc. I already did."

Raul looked curiously through the eyes of the man who called himself Al, who thought of himself as a policeman, as the metal machine on four wheels came down the street, making shrill screamings. It backed up over the curbing. Men in white examined the figure on the sidewalk, lifted him onto a stretcher and put him in the vehicle. It screamed into the distance.

Al took a small box from his jacket pocket, pressed a button and spoke with it close to his lips. He made a report and finally said, "I don't feel so great. Like maybe a headache. If it gets worse I'm going to call in and ask off."

He put the speaker back into his pocket. Raul looked out through Al's eyes at a broad street full of hurrying people and strange objects on wheels guided by other people. The people were similar in form and coloring to the people of the first world. But their clothing was different. He searched through Al's mind for words of identification and found that this city was called Syracuse, in a bigger area called New York State. The street was South Salina.

Raul also learned that Al's feet hurt, that he was thirsty, and that his "wife" had gone to visit in some faraway place. He sensed that the "wife" was a mating partner, but it was unexpectedly more than that. It was a sharing of lives as well as a mating, and a living together in a specific non-community structure called a "home." Soon he found a familiar relationship in another one of Al's random thoughts. He thought of "money," and Raul was able to identify it as the same kind of mysterious and apparently useless pieces of metal which had been pressed into his hand when he had been a water vendor on the first world. He learned that Al was given money in return for his services as a policeman, and the money went to provide food, clothing and the "home." He inserted into Al's mind the thought that no one would ever again give him any money and he was shocked by the strength of the wave of fear which followed the suggestion.

He looked through Al's eyes into the store windows, trying to guess the possible uses for objects he had never seen in any of his years in the rooms of learning. When Al looked at something of his own accord, Raul could interpret the thoughts, identify the object and learn what it was used for. A thin stick with a metal spool at one end was used to trick a creature that lived under water and was called "bass." When the hook was in the flesh of "bass," it was reeled in and lifted into the boat and later eaten. When he saw the mental picture of a bass in Al's mind, the thought of eating it made him feel queasy. When he forced Al to look at something, the man's shock and fear at finding himself doing something without awareness or purpose was so great that his mind would freeze and Raul would learn nothing.

He spent ten hours in the city, learning to more skilfully detach himself from one host and move on to the next, learning the gradations of control, from a total takeover down to that point where he could rest in a corner of the host mind and be carried about, watching and listening and comprehending, with the host unaware of his presence. He drank beer, watched part of a motion picture, drove a car and a truck and a motorbike, watched television, typed letters, washed windows, broke into a locked car and stole a camera, tried on a wedding gown in a fitting room, drilled teeth, mated, swept a sidewalk, cooked meat, played a game with a ball. He learned that one must move into a child's mind slowly and carefully, as into a small room full of fragilities, and once there one would find magical things, bright dreams and wishings. He learned that the minds of the very old ones are blurred and misted, with only the oldest memories still sharp and clear. He discovered the knack of so delicately insinuating a thought into the host mind that much could be learned from the response. Inside the mind it became a communication much like an odd conversation wherein the host mind thought it was talking to itself. Many of their thoughts were a little like dreams, in that they were yearnings and wishes and pictures of those satisfactions they wanted and did not have. Satisfactions of money and flesh and power. These were a frightened, insecure, discontented people, for the most part. They had all the violent impulses of the people in the first world, but in all their mechanized orderliness they had no way of releasing that violence. It shimmered in their minds and tore at them. They were not devoured by lions, but by their own buildings and machines. And they lived under a tyranny of "money" which seemed to Raul as cruel an oppression as that of Arrud the Elder, and as pointless.

The ten-hour dream ended, and he had tasted the minds of uncounted scores of hosts. He had awakened drained and wearied by the experience, he remembered. And he remembered also that as he had descended from the twentieth level he had passed Leesa, heading upward, and knew from her sly glance that she was on her way up to the rooms of learning. She was, at fourteen, taller than the others, ripening more quickly, but still dressed in the metallic sash of all the children of the Watchers.

Again, as after the first dream, he ate with a hunger that surprised him. Later he learned that the dreams always brought on this fierce need to fill the belly. As with the first dream, he tried to remember some of the alien words he had been able to speak while dreaming, but they were gone from his mind.

He finished and slid the eating tray back into the wall slot, hearing, as the orifice closed itself, the roaring of steam that would cleanse it for the next one to sit at that place. Two women and a man approached him as he stood up and asked him to come and sit with them in one of the talking places and tell them his dream. He went, but was so shy of his new knowledge, so obviously afraid his dream would sound both uninteresting and poorly told, that one of the women guessed the reason for his discomfort and told of her own dream first.

"I wanted to experience beauty and pain," she said, "and I chose the first world, and searched for half the dreaming before I found her. She was locked in a room of stone, and she was very weak but very beautiful. She had very strong thoughts, full of pride and hate and passion. I could not understand what they wanted her to denounce. It was some belief that had no meaning to me. I learned there was very little time left to her, and I hoped I would not have to leave her before they ended her. The men who kept her locked there tried to break her. Always one watched while the others used her. Finally she was taken in her stained rags through narrow streets. They threw filth at her. She was tied to a post and they piled things around her and a man stood in front of her and spoke in a very loud voice recounting her crimes. Then something was thrown into the substance around her, and the pain came up around her body, crackling and spitting. It was the most terrible torment I have ever found on any world, the fullest and most delicious pain. Just before her mind went dark, it became all broken lights and images and things of no meaning. When it went dark I moved into one who stood so close the red pain warmed his face, and I looked at the black sagging thing still tied to the post, and it had once been beauty, but then you could not tell what it had been. Then the dream ended."

In the silence Raul looked at the woman, Bara, saw her run the sharp pink tip of her tongue along her lips. Her eyes were shiny under the heavy lids. The glowing walls made highlights on her naked polished scalp.

One of the men smiled sadly and shook his head. "She always seeks pain and enjoys the enduring of it. Why should one want to feel what the dream creatures feel? I like best the second world. I move into the creatures and push their thoughts away. I do not want to gobble in their strange tongues. I like their darkness. I find a young strong male usually and make him crouch and wait and leap out at the weaker ones, breaking them with strong hands, running them down. The dream machines are clever. One could almost believe their screaming is real. Then they come to hunt the body I have taken. The game is to remain free until the dream ends. Sometimes there are too many of them with lights and weapons, and they break the body. Sometimes they catch it and hold it, and then I call them idiots in our own language, and they look sick with fear. These are exciting dreams." He wore a secret smile and kneaded his fingers together and nodded and nodded.

"Did you have good dreams in the first two worlds?

Did you dream well in the second world?" the other woman asked. They all stared at Raul expectantly.

He stood up. "I visited a great many in the second world. Some of them were . . . good to know, to be with in that way. And I wanted to help them and did not know how. I liked them . . . better than many I know here, among us."

The three looked astonished and then began to laugh. It was a shrill and unfamiliar sound. There was little laughter among the Watchers. "Oh, oh, oh," they cried in weakness, and the tears streamed. When at last the man could speak he stood also and rested his hand on Raul's shoulder. "We should not laugh at you. It is all new to you. The dreams seem very real the first time. But you must understand, you *dream* the creatures. You and the machine create the creatures inside your sleeping mind. When you awaken they cease to exist. It is very plain that they cease to exist, because if they did exist, they would be here, would they not? This is the only place. All else is nothingness without end."

Raul frowned at them. "There is one thing I do not know yet. Can one go back to the same world and find the same person again?"

"Yes. That is possible."

"And has he . . . lived during the time you were not dreaming of him?"

"Lived?" the other woman said. "The question does not mean anything."

"In one of my dreams can I ever dream of someone who has been in the dream of someone else?"

"It happens, but not often. It does not mean anything, Raul. It is only the cleverness of the machines turning fantastic and impossible things of the mind into three orderly worlds which seem to have chains of strange logic. But the proof is, of course, that life could not be sustained under those conditions. You will understand one day soon that it is all clever illusion, and it is there for you to enjoy now that you are no longer a child."

Bara stood, with an echo of the laughter still purring in

her throat. She plucked at a metal fold of Raul's toga. Her lips were swollen and pulpy-looking, and her voice was soft-slurred. "Raul, this is the only world. This is the place where all things are right for us. Don't let the machines delude you. Their magic is clever. Some of our people have gone mad through believing that the dream worlds are real. At last, when they begin to believe that this, the real world, is a dream, they have to be thrust out of this world. I have many reasons why I don't want that to happen to you." She tugged at his arm. "Come with me to one of the small game rooms and alone I will play for you some of the parts that I have known in dreams. You'll find it interesting."

He pulled away from her. He shouldered the man aside and walked away. At the twentieth level he looked down the row of cases. On the twentieth level the corridor walls and the floors were always dim. The brightest lights shone inside the cases themselves. Either way he looked, the cases stretched off, lining both sides of the corridor, diminishing into the distance.

He walked slowly between the cases. Many were empty. In many were dreamers. He saw Jord Orlan, hands crossed on his blue-white chest. Some were on their backs. Some curled. One woman dreamed with her arms clasped around her knees, her knees against her chest. He walked until at last he saw nothing but the empty cases, on either side of the corridor, mouth plates unused, cables coiled and waiting. The corridor turned sharply and he stared down another vista of the machines for dreaming. He walked slowly onward.

An inhabited case startled him. And then he saw that its occupant was long dead, cheeks and closed eyes shrunken into the skull, skin dark and withered. The lips were stretched back away from yellowed teeth and the teeth still loosely held the plate. One who died while dreaming, forgotten among the machines too far from the moving track to be used. When finally someone noticed that he was gone, it was probably believed that he had been properly inserted in the oval tube to speed down into the darkness.

Raul stood for a long time and looked into the case. He thought of telling Orlan, but that would entail explaining why he found it necessary to wander in unused places. This one had been dead a long time. Possibly he would never be found. He never would be inserted, head first, into the oval tube. Women were placed in the tube feet first. It was the Law.

Above his head was the soft sigh of one of the grilled apertures through which the warm air rushed. He turned and walked back to the broken track and went up in search of Leesa.

He found Leesa on a high level watching the screen where an ancient war was being fought. Sounds of battle roared from the speakers. He called to her and she turned off the machine, ran quickly to him, her eyes glowing.

She grasped his arm. "Tell me quickly! Tell me about the dreams."

He sat down, scowled up at her eager face. "Somehow, I know they are all wrong. One day you will know it too. The dreams have more meaning than . . . what they say."

"You are being absurd, Raul. They are only dreams. And it is our *right* to dream."

"A child does not speak that way to a grown one. The dreams, I say, are reality. They are as real as this floor." He stamped his bare foot.

She drew back a bit. "Don't . . . say that, Raul. Don't say it, even to me! They could put you out of the world. Through the door you told me about. And that would leave me alone here. There would be no other ugly one like me, with this hateful hair and these hideous heavy arms and legs."

He smiled at her. "I won't say it to anyone else. And you shall enjoy the dreams, Leesa. The women who look as you will look when you are grown are considered very beautiful."

She stared at him. "Beautiful? Me? Raul, I am ugly like the women in these pictures I watch."

"You will see. I promise."

She sat on her heels beside his chair. She smiled up at him. "Come, now. Tell me. You promised you would. Tell me about the dreams."

"On one condition."

"You always make conditions," she said, pouting.

"You must promise that you will help me search through all of these rooms, all of these thousands on thousands of spools. It may take us years. I do not know. But somewhere, Leesa, we shall find answers to all this. This place did not grow. It was built. What are the dreams? Why do we call ourselves the Watchers? It had to have a beginning. And somewhere, here, we will find the story of creation. Who made this world?"

"It has always been here."

"Will you help me search?" She nodded. And as she kept her eyes on his face, her lips parted, he told her of the dreams of the first two worlds.

And on the following day, he told her of the third world, as soon as his dream had ended. He saw her directly after he had reported back to Jord Orlan and had been instructed in the single Law of those who dream. He was still shaken by the significance of Jord Orlan's instruction.

She sat as before, staring up at him, rapt.

"The third world," he said, "is entirely different. The first world is all blood and cruelty. The second world is a place of nervous fear and mechanisms and intricate social patterns based on an odd sort of fear. This third world . . . I am going to return there again. Many times. Their minds are full of power and subtlety. And I know that they know of us."

"But that sounds silly, Raul! It's only a dream. How can the creatures in a dream know of the dreamers? The other ones do not."

"With the first mind I invaded, I was too cautious. There was a moment of resistance, then none. I went in confidently. While I was still moving softly, the mind thrust me away with such a surge of power I was forced to leave it. It took some time before I could find it again. This time I entered more firmly. The pressure was enormous. At last, when I took over sensory control, I saw that I was sitting in front of a small structure. The landscape was pleasant. Woods, trees, fields and flowers. There was no crudeness about the structure. The inner walls, which I could see, glowed the way these corridor walls glow. The machines in the house appeared to be automatic, much like the lower levels here. When I tried to sift the captive mind, to find out what sort of world this might be, I found nothingness. At first I thought the thing might be brainless, and then I remembered the astonishing power of the mind. I had full control of the body, but the mind itself seemed able to erect a barrier that hielded its thoughts. I looked in all directions and saw men and women, simply dressed, standing at a respectful distance and staring toward me. I stood up.

"My host let one thought seep into my mind. He told me to attempt no violence or those who watched would kill him immediately. The thoughts he transmitted to me came slowly and clearly and I had the impression he was speaking to an inferior, simplifying his thoughts for the ake of contacting a less acute mind. He told me it would ve best to return to the place from whence I came. If I attempted to move to another mind, the new host would immediately be placed in the same position in which he found himself. I formed, with his lips, our word for 'why.' He said that they could read each other's thoughts and found it relatively simple to sense an alien presence. I could detect grim humor. The others stood and watched and I began to feel that in some odd way he was still in communication with them through a channel I could not tap. I felt that he knew all about the dreams and the dreamers. I tried to make it forcefully clear that I was only curious about his world, that I intended no violence. I sat down again and he asked, again with that touch of humor, what I wanted to know."

"It sounds so dull!" Leesa said.

"It did not seem so. We spent the entire dream in talk-

ing. They call the third world Ormazd. It seems to be
named after some principle of goodness. They each live
alone, quite simply, and at a considerable distance from
one another. They give great care and attention to training and teaching their young. He seemed to 'speak' to me
as if I were a child. They live for the development and
progress of pure thought, thought independent of all emo-
tion. They have been progressing in that pattern for
twenty thousand years. The reading of minds is part of
that progress, and he told me that when they had at last
eliminated all language and all words, they had eliminated all possible misunderstanding between people. They
have no crime, no violence, no war."

"And you say it isn't dull?" Leesa asked.

"Here is what puzzles me the most. I know he knows
about us. He told me to dream about other worlds rather
than about his. But the mental word he used was not exactly 'dream.' It was more like scan, or measure or survey. I tried to question him and got that grim mental
laughter. He said we are powerless to disturb them. When
I said I was seeking knowledge, he said that it could do
no possible good to give it to me. He said it was too late.
Too late for us. He said it would be easier for me to stay
away from their world. And then in that odd laughter-of-
the-mind, there was sadness for a moment. I had the feeling he had not meant to let me see the sadness. It was
very quick, and all I got was something about a great
plan having failed. I could feel his pity. I was very glad
when I woke up at last."

"The first two worlds sound *much* better," she said.

"I can dream of any world I please now that my first
three dreams are done," he said. "I went to Jord Orlan
and he told me the Law."

"Can you tell me?"

"It is forbidden. But of course I will tell you. We both
know too many forbidden things already, Leesa. This is
the Law as he told it to me. If ever the dream creatures
on any world make machines which will take any of them

from their own world to some other world where they can live, then the dreams will end."

"Why will they end?"

"I asked that. He said that it is the Law. He said that a long time ago the first world came dangerously close to building such machines, but the Watchers obeyed the Law and caused the people of the first world to destroy their own machines time and time again until there were great explosions and now the world is a long way from building such machines. The third world has no interest in building such machines. The danger is on the second world. He said that he is afraid that too many of us have forgotten the Law. In his lifetime he has destroyed, he said, three great ships on the second world. He said we should all be dreaming in the second world, but many will dream of nothing but the first world. Jord Orlan roams the second world in every dream, looking for the great machines that will end the dreaming."

"If it is the Law," Leesa said, "then it must be done."

"Why? You and I have learned to read and to write. Only you and I can read the old records, fit the old spools to the viewing machines. Jord Orlan is firm and kind, but he no longer questions anything. He did when he was young. Now he accepts. He does not ask for reasons. That is blindness. I will know *why,* and if the reason is good, I will obey. What is the meaning of my life? Why am I here?"

"To dream?"

He could never forget the first three dreams, not even after eight years of dreams had been superimposed on those first ones.

While others dreamed their idle amusements and mischiefs and sensations, Raul had made the dreams and the waking times all a part of the same search. On the silent upper levels he spent eight years going through forgotten spools and records of all the eternity of the Watchers.

And for eight years he spent every dream in the second world, and the early dreams were always wasted when they began in some primitive place of jungle or desert, because usually then the dream would end before he could move from mind to mind a sufficient distance to reach some city where there would be libraries and laboratories. Many of the dreams were wasted in small villages until he learned the knack of thrusting upward as strongly as he could, floating in blackness, then thrusting downward and reaching out for the sense of other presences. Then as he learned the geography of the second world, he learned how to identify the area where the dream first took him, and thrust in a chosen direction for an estimated distance. Then only the first hour of ten might be wasted, but for the remainder he would be reading, through skilled and professional minds, the texts and papers on astronomy, physics, mathematics, electronics history. . . .

At last the answer came to him, shockingly, abruptly. He realized he had known it for some time but had not been able to accept it because it required such a total inversion, a turning inside out and outside in of all previous beliefs.

The answer was as blinding as a flash of intense light.

It was as unanswerable, as unarguable, as death itself.

SEVEN

RAUL KINSON KNEW THAT HE HAD TO SHARE HIS NEW knowledge with Leesa. They had grown apart since she had been permitted to dream.

He found her with a group of the younger adults. He watched her from the doorway. She had achieved the popularity, the leadership, that had been denied him. Though all thought her ugly, she was a source of constant pleasure and amusement to them.

No one could match the diabolical cleverness and inventiveness of her mind once she had taken over the hapless body of some poor citizen of world one or two. And no one could tell the dream exploits more entertainingly.

Discontent, he knew, had driven her down the more obscure pathways of the dreams, had made her vie with the others in the excesses of the dreams. She had gathered around her a group that attempted to outdo her, and always failed.

Raul listened, feeling sick at heart. In their game, each member of the group gave a short summary of their latest dream. If the group shouted approval, they would tell it in detail.

A woman said, "On the second world I found a host body on a boat. A great brute of a man. It was a small boat. I threw everyone overboard and then jumped myself. The food was left on the table. The other dream creatures will be sadly confused."

The woman pouted as no one showed disapproval. A man said, "I became the one who guides one of the big machines which go through the air. I left the controls and locked the door and stood with my back against it and watched the faces of the passengers as the machine fell strongly to the ground."

They looked at Leesa for approval. Her smile was bitter and her laugh lifted harshly over the laughter of the others. She said, "Because in the last dream I caused a great accident, you all must try to do the same thing. This last dream of mine was a small thing, but it amused me greatly."

"Tell us, Leesa. Tell us!"

"I slipped very gently into the mind of a great man of world two. A very powerful man, full of years and dignity. Over the entire ten hours of my dream, I made him count all objects aloud. The vehicles on the street, the cracks in the sidewalk, the windows in buildings. I made him count aloud and did not permit him to do anything except count aloud. His friends, his family, his co-workers, they were all horrified. The man of dignity counted until his voice was a hoarse whisper. He crawled around on his ancient knees and counted the tiles in the floor.

Doctors drugged him and I kept control of the old man's mind and kept him counting aloud. It was most amusing."

They screamed with laughter. During the next dream period Raul knew that all of them would seek variations of Leesa's latest game, but by the time they gathered to recount their dreams, Leesa would have gone on to something else.

Raul thought of the myriad lives she had broken in her attempts to prove to herself that the dreams were in no way real, but the twist of her mouth betrayed her. He knew that she still suspected that the dreams might be real, and each additional torment she inflicted on the dream creatures made more heavy the load of conscience.

In the life she led apart from the dreams and the telling of the dreams, she had nothing to do with the other adults. She was aided in this by her appearance which, though it matched standards of beauty in worlds one and two, appealed in the world of the Watchers only to those who thought to stimulate jaded tastes with the unusual.

She looked across the heads of the others and met his glance boldly. He beckoned to her and she walked slowly toward him. He went out into the corridor and she followed him. "I wish to talk to you, Leesa. It is something important."

"The dreams are important."

"We will go up to one of the rooms of learning."

She stared at him coldly. "I have not been up there in over two years. I do not intend to go up there now. If you wish to talk to me, you can meet me on the second world. We talked there once before."

He agreed reluctantly. He had a sour memory of the last time they had talked on the second world. He arranged the place and the time with her, and the recognition signal. They ate together and went up to the corridor of dreams, entered their respective cases.

He had grown almost accustomed to the clamor of the traffic, the pushing, hurrying throngs on the streets of this, the greatest city of the second world. He was late, he knew. This time it had taken almost an hour to cover half a continent. Possibly Leesa had wearied of waiting for him. She had little patience these days.

Once near the hotel he selected a lean young male body, took over the mind with a casual brusqueness that bordered on the careless. He marched the captive body into the hotel. He had thrust the host-mind far back into a corner of the captive brain. Even in panic, the struggles were weak and far away, a faint fluttering that did not interest him. There were several young women in the lobby, obviously waiting. Near the clock he took a handful of objects from the pocket of the captive body, dropped them clumsily on the floor. He bent and gathered them up—knife, change, lighter.

When he straightened up, a tall girl in gray stood before him. He looked deeply into her eyes and said, in his own tongue, "Hello, Leesa."

"You're late, Raul."

"I'm glad you waited."

They stood together and talked in low tones.

To the bystanders it appeared that a nervous young man had just arrived to meet his date. They walked out of the hotel together. She said something in the tongue of this city. Through use he had learned a great deal of it, but it was easier to relax the pressure on the host-brain, to allow it to flow up to a point where its language became his. She smiled and repeated, "Now where?"

He turned down a quieter street. He looked up across the street, saw a man and a woman standing together looking out the window of another hotel, looking down the street. "If they're alone in that room," he said, "it should be a good place."

As the gray nothingness closed around him, he made the practiced movement, slanting upward, reaching out ahead. Tendril-tips of prescience brushed another mind, tasted the blade-quick reaction of woman-mind, veered, found the other resistance point, flowed softly in.

He was standing, looking down five stories at the street.

A young couple stood on the opposite side, talking excitedly. Leesa stood beside him, and she laughed. "Let them try to explain that to each other," she said.

He looked at the small room. He pushed the captive mind down to the very thin edge of the breaking point, holding it there by an effort of will that had become almost unconscious. The body was older than the previous one. And he sensed that it was not a healthy body. It carried too much soft white weight. The woman, however, inhabited by Leesa, was beautiful in a clear-lined way.

Leesa sat on the bed. "Now be interesting, Raul."

"I intend to be. Listen closely. For six months I have had almost all the answers, almost all of our history. Now I have the last pieces. I have gotten some of it from the rooms of learning, some of it through constant questioning of the best minds of world three. And the remainder from the science of this world. A very long time ago, Leesa, a longer time than you can visualize, our world was much like this one."

"Nonsense!"

"I can prove every part of this. Our race had vast numbers. We found the secrets of travel through space. Our home planet circles a dying red sun very near a star these people call Alpha Centaurai. Twelve thousand years ago the Leaders, realizing that life could only be sustained on our home planet through a constant adjustment to the dwindling moisture and sinking temperature, directed a search for younger planets, planets suitable for migration. Three were found. This planet, also planet one, circling what these people call Delta Canis Minoris near Procyron, ten and a half light-years from here, and planet three, in the system of Beta Aquilae near Altair, sixteen light-years from this place, were found to be suitable."

"I hear the words you say, and I can find no meaning in them."

"Leesa, please listen. Twelve thousand years ago, our world was dying. The Leaders found three planets to which our people could migrate. The first world of the dreams, called Marith. This second world, Earth. The third world, Ormazd. For two thousand years the Great Migrations were the task of all our race. Ships were built which could cover the vast distances in a remarkably short time. Our race was ferried across space to the three inhabitable planets."

"But, Raul——"

"Be still until I finish. The Leaders were wise. They knew that there were three raw savage planets to be colonized, and in the colonization there would be a divergence of culture trends. They were afraid that our people, diverging in three separate directions, would become enemies. They had a choice. Either set up the colonization in such a way that there would be frequent contact between worlds, or else isolate the three colonies until such time as they had advanced to the point where contact could be reestablished without fear of conflict between them. This latter choice was selected because it was felt that by encouraging divergence, each planet would have something new to contribute to the race as a whole once contact was reestablished. In order to implement the second choice— in order to prevent premature contact between the colonial planets—the Watchers were established.

"We, Leesa, are remote descendants of the original Watchers. All the migration ships were destroyed except the six I showed you from the window. The place Jord Orlan calls our 'world' is merely a vast structure built over ten thousand years ago, when the Leaders used all the science at the disposal of our race to make it as completely automatic, as immune to time as possible. The original Watchers, five thousand in number, were selected from all the numbers of our race. They were the ones with the greatest emotional stability, the most freedom from hereditary disorders, the highest potentials of intelligence. Those original Watchers were indoctrinated with the importance of their duties, their debt to the future of the race. They were given the great building on a dying world, and six ships with which to make periodic patrols to the colonial worlds."

"But the ships are not——"

"Listen carefully. It was planned that there would be no contact between colonial worlds for five thousand years. Yet ten thousand have passed, and still it is the Law that we must prevent those 'dream' worlds from creating devices to enable them to leave their planets. Here is what happened. The structure Orlan calls our 'world' was too comfortable. Patrols were made for almost three thousand years. But those who made the patrols detested being taken out of the warmth and leisure of the structure. It had been built too well. The Watchers had not yet lost the science of the race. It took a thousand years to find a way to eliminate the physical patrols and still discharge the responsibilities given them. At last the Watchers, experimenting with the phenomenon of hypnotic control, with thought transference, with the mystery of the communication of human minds on the level of pure thought—a thing regarded as a superstition on Earth, yet practiced to the extent of near-atrophy of speech on Ormazd—devised a method of mechanically amplifying this latent ability in the human mind. The things we call dream machines are nothing more than devices which hook the massive power sources of our contrived world to the projection of thought, with three control settings so that the narrow, instantaneous beam is directed at whichever colonial world is chosen by the 'dreamer.' When we 'dream' we are but conducting a mental patrol of the actual colonial planets."

"That is absurd! You are mad!"

"For many, many years the dreams were sober, serious affairs, conducted as they were meant to be conducted. The ships sat idle. The outside world grew colder. No one left the building. The science was lost. The Watchers failed in their purpose. The genetic selection of the original Watchers was varied enough to prevent the inbreeding and resultant stagnation for five thousand years. But when the science behind the dream machines was lost, the machines themselves acquired a primitive religious significance. We have become a little colony, less than one fifth of the original number .We are blind to the true purpose of our existence. We have gone on for double the length of time originally intended. We are a curse and an affliction to the three colonial planets, merely because we believe that they do not exist, that they are something for our pleasure."

"Raul, you know that I am not here. You know that I am in the dream case which is mine for all my life, my hand under my cheek, and ——"

He went on inexorably. "We deal with three colonial planets. Marith, our favorite playground, has been turned into chronic primitive barbarism. Four thousand years ago Marith was close to space flight. We smashed them, through the dreams. There, when we possess a person, we e known as devils, as demons.

"And five thousand years ago Earth was ready for space flight. We smashed that culture, completely. When we were through, we left behind us the Aztecs, with only remnants of what had been an atomic culture. We left them with the rudiments of brain surgery, with stone pyramids shaped like the space ships they had tried to build, with sacrifices to the sun god on top of the pyramids— sacrifices actually to the hydrogen-helium reaction which they had conquered and which we had destroyed as they attempted to use it. Now Earth culture has returned to an atomic culture. We shall smash it again, drive them back into savagery. When we take over an Earth body, they have many names for us. Temporary insanity. Epilepsy. Frenzy. Trance. There are over seven hundred of us who are permitted to dream. Seven hundred feckless children who can commit acts without fear of consequence.

"On Ormazd they know who we are, and what we are. Twice we have destroyed their attempts to cross space. They no longer have the urge to leave their planet. They have found vaster galaxies within the human mind than any that can be conquered by machines. All three colonial planets would be better rid of us, Leesa."

In a halting voice she said, "I have tried to believe you.

But I cannot. Were I to believe you, it would mean that . . ."

"You might have to accept a moral responsibility for the acts you have committed, for death you have brought to people as real as you and I?"

"We are in the dream cases, Raul. The clever machines make this world for us."

"Then break that mirror. Tomorrow you can return to find it broken. Or dive from that window. Tomorrow you can return to find the broken body of the girl you are inhabiting."

"That is because of the cleverness of the machines."

"There are other proofs, Leesa. On Ormazd you can find the records of the original Migrations. On Marith you can read their mythologies, and find reference to the ships that landed, belching fire. They think they came from the sun. On Earth here, a race believes themselves descended from the sun. And there are traces, in Earth mythology, of giants that walked the earth, of great ships and chariots that crossed the sky. All three planets were populated by manlike creatures before our remote ancestors arrived. On Earth, after a time, the two races could interbreed. On Marith and Ormazd the original races died out. You see, Leesa, there is too much proof to be ignored."

She was silent for a long time. "I cannot believe what you say. Tomorrow I shall enclose myself in the case. I shall become a naked savage girl in a jungle, or a woman leading a burro down a mountain path. Or I can meet with my friends on Marith and we can play the game of identification, or the game of killing, or the game of love, or the game of the chase. No, Raul. No. I cannot change what I believe."

"Leesa," he said softly, "you have always believed, in your heart, that these worlds are real. That is why you have been so wanton, so cruel, in your dreams, because you were trying to deny their existence. You and I are different. We are not like the others. We are stronger. You and I can change the——"

He stopped speaking as he saw the woman on the bed put her hand to her forehead and look at him oddly. She spoke so slowly that even without releasing the host, he understood her. "George, I feel so strange."

Leesa had gone. He knew not in what direction. She had ended the talk in such a way that he could not find her. He let the host-mind take over the maximum amount of control, right on the edge of the fading of vision and hearing which would mean a full release of the host.

"Something wrong with those drinks, maybe. That bartender had a funny look. Maybe it was a mickey. I feel funny too."

The woman lay back on the bed. Raul felt the slow beginning of desire in the host-body. The woman smiled up at him. As the man moved toward the bed Raul released the last of his control, faded off into the familiar area where there was no color, no light. Nothing but the strange consciousness of direction. He slanted downward with a gentle impulse, drifting until he felt the nearby entity, orienting himself to it, gathering it in slowly. Vision came. He was in a taxi. He was late. The host-mind was fogged with alcohol, but the emotions were particularly vivid. Raul read the mind as one might turn the pages of a book. Despair and torment and the desire for death. Hate, fear and envy. But most of all an enormous longing for a sleep that would be endless. The man paid the driver, walked slowly into a lobby, took the small self-service elevator up to the eighth floor. He unlocked the door and went in. The woman came out of the bedroom with the shining weapon in her hand. She pointed it and shut her eyes. The little hot bits of lead bit warm liquid channels into the host-body—not pain. Just shock and warmness and a sort of melting. The host-brain faded quickly, and as Raul slid away, he caught the last impulse of consciousness. Not satisfaction with the surprise gift of the death that had been desired—but panic and fear and longing for the things of life as yet untasted.

Raul did not find ease of spirit until at last he entered

the mind of a man, an old man, who sat in the park, half dozing in the sun. In that mind he waited for the dream to end.

EIGHT

IN THE PRIVATE ROOMS ASSIGNED TO HIM BECAUSE HE was Leader, Jord Orlan stared at the girl who sat facing him, hoping to disconcert her with his silence. This Leesa Kinson was too . . . alive. The heavy strands of black hair were unusual. Hair like that of the dream people, or like that of her brother, Raul. The planes of her face had strength and her lips were too red. Jord Orlan preferred the quieter, drabber, frailer women. With an effort he brought his memory back to the reason for summoning her to him.

"Leesa Kinson, it has been reported to me that you have had no child."

"That is right."

"It has been reported that you have favored no man among us."

She smiled as though it were of no consequence. "Perhaps no one finds me acceptable. I have been told that I am remarkably ugly."

"You smile. Have you forgotten the Law? Too many of the women are barren. All who can have a child must do so. It is the duty of all to have a child. You are as strong as a man. It is the Law that you must have many children. The weak ones too often die, and the child with them."

"You talk about the Law. Where is the Law? Can I handle it, read it?"

"Reading is a habit of the first and second worlds. Not here."

Her lip curled. "I can read. I learned when I was a child

on the high levels. My brother taught me. I can read our language and I can write it. Show me the Law."

"The Law was told to me. It was told enough times so that I remember it and even now I am teaching it to others. I had hoped to teach it to Raul but——"

"He has no interest in being Leader. Is it against your Law to learn to read?"

"I find you impertinent. It is my Law and also yours, Leesa Kinson. To learn to read is not against the Law. It is merely pointless. What is the reason for reading? There are the dreams and the food and sleep and the rooms for games and healing. Why read?"

"It is good to know something that others do not know, Jord Orlan."

"If you persist in impertinence I shall punish you by denying you the right to dream for many many days."

She shrugged and regarded him steadily. Her gray eyes made him oddly uncomfortable. He said more gently, "The old ways are the best ways. Why are you not happy?"

"Who is?"

"Why, I am! All of us are. Life is full. You and Raul are the discontented ones. The strange ones. When I was small there was one like you two. In fact, I believe that he may have been the father of your mother. He, too, had a different appearance. He created much trouble, and was punished many times. He struck many of the men, and he was hated and feared. Then one day a woman saw him just as he climbed into the oval tube that leads down into the unending blackness. She had no wish to stop him. You see, that is the end of discontentment. You must learn to be contented."

Her eyelids grew heavy and she yawned. It angered him.

He leaned forward. "Leesa Kinson, I believe that this attitude of yours is unnatural. I believe that it was caused by your brother. He has been a bad influence. He has nothing to do with any of the games. When he is not dreaming, it is impossible to find him."

An idea began to shape itself. He considered it carefully. "May I go?" she asked.

"No. I am curious about your brother. I have attempted to talk to him many times. No one knows of his dreams. He does not enter into any of the games. I suspect him of neglect of the prime responsibility of the dream. Has he talked to you of . . . of any matters which could be considered heresy?"

"Would I tell you?"

"I think you might be glad to. I am not vindictive. If his ideas are incorrect I shall attempt to change them. If you refuse to give me any information, I shall order you to favor a man of my own choosing, one who will follow orders. It is within my power to do that. And it is the Law that you shall bear children."

Her lips were compressed. "Orders can be disobeyed."

"And you can be taken to a place on the lowest level and thrust out of this world for failure to disobey an order. I would not care to do that. So tell me what Raul has said to you."

She moved a bit in the chair, not meeting his glance. "He . . . he has said things that are not right."

"Go on."

"He has said that the three worlds of the dreams actually exist and that what we call dreams are just . . . a method for us to visit the three real worlds. He says that this world is just a big structure and that it rests on a planet that is like the other three, but colder and older."

Jord Orlan stood up quickly and began to pace back and forth. "It is more serious than I believed. He needs help. Badly. He must be made to see the Truth."

"The Truth as you see it?" she asked gently.

"Do not scoff. What did you say when Raul told you his absurd theories?"

"I told him that I didn't believe him."

"Very good, my child. But now you must go to him and you must pretend to believe what he says. You must encourage him to say more. You must find out what he does, in his dreams. And you must report everything back to me immediately. When we know the full extent of his heresy we will be in a better position to take his hand and lead him to the Truth." His voice grew more resonant. He faced her, his arms spread, his face glowing. "Once, when I was young, I doubted too. But as I grew wiser, I found the Truth. The entire universe is encompassed within these familiar walls. Outside is the end of all, an unthinkable emptiness. Our minds cannot comprehend utter emptiness. It is a thousand times less than the floating just before you enter the mind of a dream creature. In this universe, this totality, there are nearly one thousand souls. We are the static nub of the universe, the only small place of reality. It has been thus forever, and forever shall be. Now go and do as I say, Leesa."

As she went to the doorway she remembered what Raul had told her the day before she was first permitted to dream. "If a small living creature is put in a white box before its eyes are open, if it lives out its life in that box, if food and warmth are provided, and if it dies in that box —then, in the moment of death, the little creature can stare at the walls of the box and say 'This is the world.'"

His words had come back to her an uncomfortable number of times.

She found Raul on one of the highest levels. The micro-book page at which he stared was incomprehensible to her. He heard the soft sound of her bare feet against the floor and turned, startled.

He smiled. "A long time since you've come up here, Leesa. I haven't seen you since you interrupted our talk."

He clicked off the projector. "What were you looking at?" she asked.

He stood up and stretched. His expression was sour. "At something I'll never understand, I'm afraid. This box contains all of the texts used by the technicians who piloted the Migration ships. I only found them by accident. I could look for the rest of my life and not find the intermediary texts. The science is beyond me. In the old days it was beyond any individual man too. They were organized into work teams and research teams. Each man handled one part of a particular problem and all of the work was coordinated through the use of integral calculators. But maybe I can——" He stopped suddenly.

She sat in one of the other chairs. "Can what?"

"Maybe I can find out enough so that I can handle one of the patrol ships. I know the interior details of the ships now."

"What good would that be?"

"I could go to one of the three worlds. I could take some of them onto the ship and bring them back here and bring them into this tower and show them to Orlan and the others. Then they'd stop this childish babbling about the Law, and about this being the only true reality. There are men on Earth who could look at a patrol ship, one man in particular who could learn much from one, so that even if I were unable to return, he would be able to . . . I talk too much."

"Maybe I find it interesting."

"You didn't a short time ago."

"Couldn't I have thought it over?" she said, pouting.

There was excitement in his tone. "Leesa! Are you beginning to see what I've seen for so long?"

"Why not? Maybe I could . . . help you."

He frowned. "You might, at that. I'd about given up hope of ever . . . Never mind. I guess I should trust you." He looked directly into her eyes. "Do you understand now that you've spent six years smashing the lives of people who actually exist, who exist and go about their affairs while we're talking here? Do you believe that?"

She held the chair arms tightly. "Yes," she said, as calmly as she could.

"I told you that we've outlived our purpose. If nothing were done we'd eventually disappear, but we'd go on and on, striking like random lightning into the lives of men until the very end, making public figures do dangerous and incomprehensible things, making obscure little men and women commit acts that baffle their courts, confound their friends and ruin their lives. I am going to put an end to it."

"How, Raul?"

"Marith is too primitive for space travel—Ormazd too concerned with the human mind to be mechanistic. Earth is my hope. There is a man there who is in charge of a project to build a space ship which is quite like those I showed you from the window. Since so many odd accidents—which we can explain and they can't—have happened to all previous attempts, this one is being handled with the greatest secrecy. With eleven billion host-minds to choose from, roughly, the less than eight hundred Watchers are unlikely to find this project, even though it is in an area where we have ruined previous projects. I am trying to protect that project and I am trying to get into more direct contact with a man named Bard Lane who is in charge. I want to explain what has happened to previous projects and assure him of my desire to help, and warn him against what one of us might do while dreaming. Not long ago someone stumbled across the project, possessed one of the technicians and spoiled months of work. I haven't been able to find out who it was. They haven't been back, but they may come back. I can't go and talk to the others. It would arouse suspicion, because it would be something I haven't done in years. But you might be able to find out, Leesa."

"And if I should find out?"

"Tell the person who possessed the technician that you stumbled on the same project and destroyed it utterly. In order to do that convincingly, you should . . ."

"Why do you pause?"

"Can I trust you? Somehow, you do not seem sufficiently . . . shattered by the realization that in the dream worlds we are dealing with reality. The day when I was at last convinced, I thought for a time that I might go mad. I wanted to go up to the corridor of dreams and rip all the cables free, smash all the dials."

"You can trust me," she said evenly.

"Then, in order to convince the person who did the damage, you should take a look at the project. It is called Project Tempo. I will explain to you exactly how to find it. It is quite difficult because of the lack of contacts in the surrounding countryside. I have been most successful through using the drivers of vehicles, and it is a matter of luck to emerge near a road. The last time it took me so long that I had but a little more than an hour to . . . do what I planned."

"What are you doing when you go there?"

"Explaining to Bard Lane just what we are."

"How do you find it?"

"Before I tell you, I must have your solemn promise that you will do no damage to the project. Do you promise?"

"I will do no damage," she said, and in her thoughts she added, on the first visit, at least.

He opened a case on the floor. "Here," he said, "is a map I made here after committing it to memory on Earth."

She knelt beside him. She watched his finger trace the possible routes of entry to the project area.

NINE

DR. SHARAN INLY SAT AT HER DESK, HER HANDS PRESSED against her eyes, her fingernails digging into her forehead just below the hair line. She wished with all her heart that she had become a stenographer, or a housewife, or a welder.

You could deal with humans, and be interested in them as humans even when they were cases duplicating those in the texts. Yet, as you treated them, you kept a tiny bit of yourself in reserve. It was self-protection. And then you would run into a case that would break your heart, because somehow you had gotten too involved with the individual as a person, not as a case.

"I hope you've got an explanation," Bard Lane said coldly as he slammed into her office.

"Shut the door and sit down, Dr. Lane," she said with a tired smile.

He sat down. His face had a drawn look. "Dammit, Sharan, my desk is piled high. Adamson needs help. The fool committee that wants to administer the death kiss to this whole project is waiting. I know you can bring anyone here at any time, but I think you might have checked first. Just a little consideration for the amount of work I——"

"How did you sleep last night?"

He stared at her, stood up with determination. "Fine, and I eat well, too. I even take walks. Want me to make a muscle for you?"

"Sit down, Dr. Lane!" she said crisply. "I'm doing my job. Please cooperate."

He sat down slowly, a look of fear in his eyes, growing fear. "What is this, Sharan? I guess I slept well enough. I felt tired this morning, though."

"What time did you get to bed?"

"A little before midnight. I was up at seven."

"Thomas Bellinger, on the routine guard report, noted that you went into your office at ten minutes after two this morning."

Bard gasped. "The man's mad! No! Wait a minute. If somebody could plant a man who looks like me . . . Have you alerted all guards?"

She slowly shook her head. Her eyes were on him. "No, Bard. That won't work. You passed the full test series with flying colors just this week, but it still won't work. You noticed that Bess Reilly wasn't in your office this morning?"

He frowned. "She's sick today. She phoned from her quarters."

"She phoned from here, Bard. I asked her to. Bess was a little behind in her work. She went in early this morning. She went into your office and took yesterday's tape off the dictation machine and took it out to her desk to transcribe it. When she started to listen to it, she thought you were playing some sort of joke. She listened some more and it frightened her. She very properly brought it directly to me. I've been over it twice. Would you care to hear it?"

He said softly, "Dictation . . . a funny nightmare is coming back to me, Sharan. Silly thing, like most of them are. It seems I had something that I had to get down before it went out of my mind. And I dreamed I . . ."

"Then you walked in your sleep, Bard. Listen to what you said."

She moved the small speaker closer to his chair, depressed the switch on the playback machine.

It was unmistakably Bard Lane's voice. "Dr. Lane, I am taking this method of communicating with you. Do not be alarmed and do not doubt me. I am physically nearly four and a half light-years from you at this moment. But I have projected my thoughts into your mind and I hav taken over your body to serve the purposes of the mo ment. My name is Raul Kinson and I have been watching your project for some time. I am anxious for it to succeed, as it is your world's only chance to free itself from those of us whose visitations are unprincipled, who only want to destroy. I do not want to destroy. I want to help you create. But there are dangers that I can warn you about, dangers which you do not, as yet, understand. Take warning from what h ppened when your technician, Kornal, was seized by one of us. We are the survivors on your parent planet. I do not wish to tell you too much at this moment. Be assured that my intentions are friendly. Do not b alarmed. Do not fall into the logical error of assuming tha this is an indication of mental unbalance. I will attempt t communicate with you in a more direct manner a bit later. Hear me out when I do."

Sharan clicked the switch to the off position. "You see?" she said softly. "The same delusion as before. This is just a further refinement of it. I'm both glad and sorry that Miss Reilly brought it to me. But here it is, Bard. Now do you think I should have sent for you?"

"Of course," he whispered. "Of course."

"What am I to do?" Sharan asked.

"Do your job," he said. His mouth was a hard, bloodless line.

Her voice was dispassionate, but her hand trembled as

she handed him the note previously prepared. "This will admit you for observation. I see no need to assign an orderly to you while you pack what you'll need. I'll advise Adamson that he's acting chief until you're replaced."

He took the note and left her office without a word. After he closed the door softly behind him, she buried her face in the crook of her arm, her shoulders hunched over the desk. She pounded gently on the desk top with her clenched left fist.

Bard Lane walked from the hospital lounge into his room at the end of the corridor. He wore the beltless bathrobe they had issued to him, the soft plastic slippers. He lay on the bed and tried to read the magazine he had carried in from the lounge. It was a news digest, and seemed to contain nothing except hollow-sounding absurdities.

New Navy sub successfully withstands the pressure at the deepest point of the Pacific. Mello Noonan, creamy-tressed star of video, lands her heli-cycle on the observation deck of the new Stanson Building, smilingly pays the forty-dollar fine. Russians, through careful research, prove that man first walked erect at a spot fourteen miles east of present-day Stalingrad. Teen-age girls in Houston set new fad by shaving their heads and painting them green. When they meet on the street, they doff shoes and 'shake hands' with their feet. Memphis musician brains girlfriend with tuba. Widow in Victoria, Texas, claims to be receiving spirit messages from long-dead Valentino. Georgia ax killer claims, at trial, that he was 'possessed'—accusing mother-in-law of putting the evil eye on him. Injunctions issued against further use of new Reno slot machines which provide divorce papers for a fifty-dollar fee. Doctors unable to bring nine-year-old twins in Daytona out of trance caused by forty-one hours spent in front of their home video screen. Vote fraud in North Dakota . . . dope ring indicted . . . gambling ship sunk . . . bride leaves third grade . . . multiple murder . . . drives car into shoppers . . . jumped from eighty-third floor . . . minister fires church . . . dresses four inches shorter next year

. . . curb service vice . . . hate . . . fear . . . anger . . .
envy . . . lust . . .

He lay back on the bed. The magazine slipped to the
floor, landing with the dry sound of a dead winged thing.
Madness in the world. Madness tolling in his mind like a
huge cracked bell in a forgotten tower, a bell swayed by
the unknown winds. He shut his hands hard, squeezed his
eyes shut and felt his soul as a fading focal point of certainty in this alien body, in this body of webbed nerves
and muscle fiber and convoluted brain. He knew that any
idea of plan or order in this mad world was pure delusion,
that man was a tiny creature, knotted with the most deadly
instincts, that he could look at the stars, but never attain
them. In the back of his mind he stood at the edge of a
distorted cliff, and he leaned toward the darkness. So easy
to fall, to drop downward with a scream so vast and so
solid that it would be as a smooth silver column inserted
slickly in his throat. He would fall with his head tilted
back, his lips drawn wide, with white-rimmed iris, with
long tortured spasm that . . .

The bed moved. He opened his eyes. The little blond
nurse from the lounge sat on the end of his bed. The stiff
starched uniform had a bold life of its own, as though, inside it, her tender body recoiled from any touch against its
harshness. The temple veins were violet tracery against
the luminescent skin. Her large eyes were blue-purple
glass beads from a costume jewelry counter.

"As bad as that, Bard Lane?" she said.

He frowned. Nurses were not supposed to sit on pa-
tients' beds. Nurses did not speak with such casual informality. Possibly in the psych ward the nurses had special
leniency from the rigid rules applying to those who nursed
more obvious wounds.

"Maybe I can do a soft-shoe dance to show how gay I
am," he said.

"He didn't tell me about you. I thought I'd take a look
while he's getting you out of here. Of course, he might not
approve."

"Who are you talking about, Nurse? And what didn't he tell you, whoever he is?"

"Nurse is so formal. My name is Leesa."

"Very odd name. And you seem like an odd girl. I don't follow you very well, Leesa."

"I don't imagine that you'll be able to, Bard Lane. Actually I was talking about Raul, my brother, if that means anything. Raul Kinson."

Lane sat up, his face flushed with anger. "Nurse, I'm not so far gone that I'm going to stand still for any half-baked experiments. Go on back to Sharan and tell her that it didn't work. I'm still rational."

The nurse tilted her blond head to one side and smiled. "I like you when you're angry, Bard Lane. So fierce! Anyway, Raul is sorry that he got you into this mess by being too anxious to get into communication with you. Now he's trying to straighten things out for you. Poor Raul! He thinks that you actually exist. All of you people are so obsessed with the idea of your own reality. It gets tiresome."

Bard stared at her. He said slowly, "Nurse, this is just friendly advice from a patient. Why don't you go to Dr. Inly and ask to have the standard series? You know, when a person works around . . . mental cases for a long enough time, it sometimes happens that——"

Her laugh was raw gold, and oddly sane. "G— — — So solemn and so kindly! In a minute you'll be patting me on the head and kissing my forehead."

"If this approach of yours is supposed to help me, Nurse, I . . ."

She became serious. "Listen to me. You're just part of an unpleasant and rather dull dream as far as I'm concerned. Raul seems to get a certain amount of amusement out of fooling himself about you. I wanted to see what you looked like. He seems very impressed with you. But I don't have to be. I . . ."

A stocky woman in white appeared in the open doorway. She scowled. "Anderson! What is the meaning of this? Number seventeen has been signaling for the last ten minutes. And I've been trying to find you. You know better than to sit on a patient's bed. I'm sorry this happened, Dr. Lane, but——"

The little blond nurse gave the supervisor a solemn wink. She slid up toward the head of the bed, curled a soft arm around Lane's neck and kissed him firmly and warmly on the lips. The supervisor gasped.

The little blond nurse straightened up. Slowly a look of horror came over her face. She jumped to her feet, holding her hands at her breast, twisting her fingers until her knuckles cracked.

"I demand an explanation, Anderson," the supervisor said ominously.

"I . . . I . . ." Two tears spilled over her lower eyelids and ran down her cheeks. She backed away from the bed.

"I think Leesa is a little upset," Bard said. His tone was placating.

"Her name is Elinor," the supervisor said crisply.

The nurse turned and fled. The supervisor sighed. "More trouble. I'm shorthanded, and now I'll have to send her up for tests." She plodded out of the room.

Sharan Inly was staring at Major Tommy Leeber. His smooth, jocular voice was just the same, his oval face kindly, his eyes jet-hard. But his words made Sharan feel a distant thunder in her ears, a weakness that was like the lethargy that came before a dead faint.

"If this is some sort of stupid joke, Major——"

"I'll start from the beginning again, Dr. Inly. I made a mistake. But you made one also. My name is Raul Kinson. For the moment I am using the body of this man named Leeber. That shouldn't be too difficult to accept as a basic premise. I used Lane's body and sent him a message. Both you and Lane apparently jumped to the conclusion that he is mentally unsound."

"I think General Sachson would like to have Lane and myself off the project, Major Leeber. I don't care for your way of trying to eliminate me."

"Please, Dr. Inly. There must be some test we can

make. If I could repeat the message that I left for Lane to find——"

"Bess Reilly could have told you the message."

"I don't know who she is, but please have her come in and ask her."

They waited. Bess Reilly arrived within a few moments. She was a very tall girl, angular and without beauty, except for her eyes, sea-green, long-lashed, expressive.

"Bess, have you spoken to anyone about that dictation tape on Dr. Lane's machine?"

Bess lifted her chin a fraction of an inch. "Dr. Inly, you told me not to tell anyone. And I didn't. I'm not the sort to——"

"Have you talked to Major Leeber today?"

"I saw him once yesterday for the first time. I've never spoken to him."

Sharan gave the girl a long, steady look. "Thank you, Bess. You can go."

The door closed behind her. She turned to Major Leeber. "Now tell me what the tape said."

Leeber repeated it. In two places he made minor changes in sentence structure, but the rest of it was completely accurate. There was a calmness and a confidence about him that disturbed her.

She said, "Major, or Raul Kinson, or whoever you are . . . I . . . this is something that I can't bring myself to believe. This idea of taking over other people. This idea of coming from some alien planet. There are cases on record where persons have repeated the contents of sealed envelopes. You'll have to do better."

"Bard Lane has to be put back in charge. I am going to have to frighten you, Dr. Inly. But it will be the best proof I can give you. Without attempting to explain how, I am going to vacate this host brain and enter your brain. In the process, Major Leeber will revert to complete consciousness. But he won't remember very much of what has gone on. I will use your voice to get rid of him."

Sharan's smile felt as though it had been painted across her lips with a stiff brush. "Oh, come now!"

She sat with her palms pressed flat and hard against the cool desk top. The idea, in spite of its preposterousness, gave her an odd feeling of shame, as though an alien invasion of her mind would be a violation more basic than any physical relationship could ever be. Her mind had been a temple, a place of refuge, a place of secret thoughts, some of them so abandoned as to cause, in someone without her knowledge of psychiatry, a sense of guilt. To have these secret places laid bare would be . . . like walking naked through the streets of a city.

She saw the shock on Leeber's face, his confused look around the office, the way he rubbed the back of his hand across his mouth. And then she had no more time to watch Leeber. She felt the probe of unseen tendrils. She felt their softness. She tried to resist. Memory fled back to a time years before. A slushy day in a northern city. She had been playing in the gutter with the boy from next door. The water from the melting snow ran swiftly down the slope. They had built dams out of snow to contain it. But it would not be contained. It snaked around the dams, ate through them, thrusting always forward with gentle inevitability.

She moved back and back, seeking a last defensive point. And suddenly there was the sensation of the entire entity within her brain, adjusting itself to the familiar neural patterns, settling itself in a way that was oddly like the manner in which a dog, before sleeping, will turn around and around.

Words had always been planned a few seconds in advance. Her lips parted and the knowledge of the meaning of her words was simultaneous with the utterance of the words themselves.

"The sun is bad here, Major. It has made you a little dizzy. Drink a lot of water today and take salt tablets. You can get them at the dispensary. Stay out of the sun and you'll be all right by morning."

Leeber stood up. "Uh . . . thanks," he said. He paused at the door, looked back at her with a puzzled expression, shook his head and went out.

The thought came to her. It was not written out inside her mind. It was not expressed in words, and yet the words formed to match the thought. "Now you understand? Now you believe? I will relax controls. To communicate with me, speak aloud."

"I've gone mad!"

"That is what the others think. No. No, you're not insane, Sharan. Watch your hand."

She looked down. Her head reached out and took a pencil. It moved over toward the scratch pad. Without volition, she wrote her own name. "Sharan." And then the room dimmed and faded and she knew nothing. As sight came back she saw that she had written another word under her own name. At least she imagined that it was a word.

"Yes, a word, Sharan. Your name in my own writing. I had to force you far back away from the threshold of consciousness in order to write it."

It was written with bolder strokes than her own handwriting. It looked as Arabic might look if written with cursive style rather than individual word signs.

"Mad, mad, mad," she said aloud.

Anger in her mind. Alien anger. "No. Don't be a fool! Believe! Wait, Sharan. I'll find your thoughts and your beliefs. I'll learn all there is to know of you, Sharan."

"No," she said.

She sat rigid, and tiny soft combs moved through all parts of her mind. Memory came to her, days long passed, hopelessly cluttered and out of sequence. The music at her mother's funeral. A passage from her doctor's thesis. A man's insistent lips. The song she wrote once. Discontent. Pride in her profession. Endless minutes and she felt as though she were pinned flat on a vast specimen board . . .

"Now I know you, Sharan. I know you well. Now do you believe?"

"Mad."

No more anger. Resignation. Fading. Gone—dwindling slowly away, a song half heard in the far sweet dusk of summer.

She sat alone. She pulled open a drawer, took out one of the slips like the one she had given to Bard Lane. She started to fill it in. Name. Symptoms. Partial diagnosis. Prognosis.

The door opened and Jerry Delane, the young dispensary doctor, came in. She frowned at him and said, "Isn't it customary to knock, Dr. Delane?"

He sat down facing her across the desk. He said, "I told you that I would leave Leeber's mind and enter yours, and I did. Of course you can call me a fantasy your sick mind has dreamed up, so I'll give you physical proof." He pulled her dictating machine toward him, set the switch, smiled at her and spoke into it. "Fantasies cannot record their words, Sharan."

To Sharan, the light seemed to fade in the room with the exception of the light around his smiling mouth. It seemed to grow larger, rushing toward her, overpoweringly large. And then it was as though she were moving swiftly toward the smile. Roaring down a tunnel toward the white even teeth, the murderous redness of the lips . . .

She was on the leather couch and he was kneeling beside her. He held a cold wet compress against the left side of her forehead. His eyes were tender.

"What . . ."

"You fainted and fell. You toppled against the edge of the file cabinet."

She frowned. "I . . . I think I'm ill, Jerry. I had odd thoughts . . . delusions about——"

He stilled her words with a gentle finger against her lips. "Sharan, please. I want you to believe me. I am Raul Kinson. You must believe me."

She stared at him. Slowly she pushed the hand away from her forehead. She walked to the desk, wavering slightly. She switched the dictation machine to play back, set it a fraction ahead. The voice, thin and metallic, said, "Fantasies cannot record their words, Sharan."

She turned and faced him. In a dead voice she said, "I believe you now. There is no choice, is there? No choice at all."

"No choice. Release Bard Lane. Get him over here. The three of us will talk."

They sat and waited for Bard Lane. Raul stared at her. He said softly, "Odd, odd."

"You can use that word?"

"I was thinking of your mind, Sharan. I have avoided the minds of women. They have all had a shifting, unfocused, intuitive pattern. Not your mind, Sharan. Every facet and phase seemed . . . familiar to me. As though I have always known you. As though your every emotional response to any situation would be the feminine parallel of my own reaction."

She looked away from him. "You haven't left me much privacy, you know."

"Is privacy necessary? I know of a world where words are not used. Where a man and a woman, mated, can dwell within each other's minds at will. They have true closeness, Sharan. In your mind I found . . . another reason for making certain that this project succeeds."

She felt annoyance as the flush made her cheeks feel warm. "This is a brand new approach," she said with acid tone. "Maybe you'd like to fingerprint me too."

Bess Reilly came in. She slammed the door, yawned, hitched her bony hips onto the edge of the desk. She grinned at Jerry and said lazily, "Time's running short, Raul. And I can't say I'm sorry. You don't have much fun in your dreams, do you? I've had to change hosts forty times to find you again."

"I felt you near a few moments ago," Raul said. He turned to Sharan. "I present my sister, Leesa Kinson."

Sharan looked blankly at Bess Reilly's familiar face. Bess stared at her. She said, "Does she believe you, Raul?"

"Yes, she does."

"It gives me a funny feeling to have one of them understand how it is with us. I never had it happen before. Once, for a gag, I tried to make a man understand who I was when I took over the body of his bride. It took him just about an hour and a half to go crazy. I haven't tried since. That is, until today. I took over a little blond nurse and tried to introduce myself to your friend, Bard Lane. He got a bit confused. Are you in any danger of going crazy, girl?"

"Yes," Sharan said. "If this keeps up."

Bess laughed. "Don't take yourself too seriously."

Bard Lane came in slowly and shut the door behind him. He glanced curiously at Jerry Delane and Bess Reilly. He addressed himself to Sharan. "You sent for me."

"This is your old friend, Leesa," Bess said. "How did the little nurse act after I moved away from her?"

Sharan saw the color leave Bard's face. She spoke hurriedly. "Bard, we were wrong. Just believe me. They've proven it to me. It is impossible, I know. But it's true. Some sort of long-range hypnosis, I guess. But there is a Raul Kinson. He had . . . he is using Jerry Delane's body. He wants to talk to us. And his sister, Leesa, is . . . Bess is Leesa. Jerry and Bess won't remember what has happened. That recording you made. Everything is true, Bard. I think one moment I've gone mad and the next moment I know it's the truth."

Bard Lane dropped heavily into a chair and held his hand across his eyes. No one spoke. When at last he looked up, his expression was bleak. He stared at Jerry. "What is this test you have to say to me?"

Speaking slowly, pausing at times, Raul Kinson told of the Watchers, the Leaders, the Migrations, the dream machines, and of the perversion, over fifty centuries, of what had once been a logical plan. He told of the one Law which governed all of those who dreamed.

Bess sat on the edge of the desk, a bored look on her face.

Bard looked down at the knuckles of his clenched fist. "And so," he said softly, "if we can believe you, you give us the answer to why, with most of the techniques under control, every attempt to conquer deep space has been a miserable failure."

There was no answer. He looked up. Jerry Delane stood

with an odd expression on his face. "What am I doing in here? How did I get in here?"

Bess slid quickly off the desk. "Did you call me, Dr. Inly?" she asked in a shrill, frightened voice.

Sharan forced a smile. "The conference is over, kids. You can go. You will stay, Bard?"

Jerry and Bess left the office.

"Have we gone mad?" Bard asked.

"There is no such thing as shared delusion, mutual fantasy, Bard," Sharan said in a tired voice. "And either you are still in the ward and all this is taking place in your mind—or else I have gone off completely and I only imagine you are here. Or, what seems the most difficult of all —it is all true." She stood up. "Dammit, Bard! If I close my mind to this thing, it means that my mind is too little and too petty to encompass it. But try—just try—to swallow this tale of alien worlds, Leaders, Migrations. No, it won't wash. I have a better idea."

"Which I will be delighted to hear."

"Sabotage. A new and very clever variety. Some of our friends on the other side of this world have managed to develop hypnotic technique to a new level of efficiency. Maybe they use some form of mechanical amplification. They're trying to discredit us if they can't drive us mad. That has to be it."

Lane frowned. "If their technique is that good, why do it the hard way? Why not just take over Adamson and Bill Kornal and a few other key men and have them spend a few hours damaging the Beatty One?"

"You forget. They already took over Kornal. It gave them a few months of grace. Now they're experimenting. Maybe they will try to talk us into leaving here and going to another country. You can't tell what they have in mind. Bard, the one who calls himself Raul Kinson warned me that he was going to enter my mind. And then he did. It was . . . degrading and horrible. We've got to get in touch with our own people who might know something about this. Maybe some of the ESP men. And then there's Lurdorff. He's done some amazing things with hypnosis. Hemorrhage control. That sort of thing. Why are you looking at me like that?"

"I'm trying to picture just how you'd state the problem without ending up on the receiving end of some fancy shock therapy, Sharan."

She sat down slowly. "You're right," she said. "There's no way we can warn them. No way in the world."

TEN

LEESA, WALKING DOWN ONE OF THE LOWER LEVELS, SAW Jord Orlan step off the moving ramp, glance at her and look quickly away. She lengthened her stride to catch him.

"I have something to tell you," she said.

He looked nervously down the corridor.

"It's all right. Raul has gone up to the unused levels."

"Come then," he said. He led the way to his quarters, walked in ahead of her. When he turned around he saw that she was already seated. He frowned. The respectful ones waited to be asked.

"I have been expecting a report, Leesa Kinson."

"Raul trusts me. Perhaps, too much. It makes me feel uncomfortable."

"Remember, this is for his own good."

"I've had to pretend to be very contrite for all the damage I've caused in the dream worlds to all those precious little people he thinks are actually alive."

Jord Orlan forgot his annoyance with her. "Very good, child! And have you shared his dreams?"

"Yes. He explained how he found a space ship project by searching the mind of a certain colonel in Washington. He told me how to find the project. We met there, in host bodies. Raul seems very proud of the people who work there. He wants to protect the project against . . . us. Not long ago the project was damaged by one of us who came across it, probably by accident, and forced a technician to smash delicate equipment. Raul does not want that to happen again."

"How does he hope to prevent it?"

"He has told two of them about the Watchers, and he has managed to prove to them that we exist."

Jord Orlan gasped. "That is a paradox! To convince someone who does not exist of existence on the only true plane. Many of us have amused ourselves trying to tell the dream people about the Watchers. They invariably go mad."

"These two did not. Possibly because the woman is an expert on madness and the man is . . . strong."

He stared at her. "Do not fall into the trap in which your brother finds himself. When you spoke of the man you looked as though you might believe him to be real. He is merely a figment of the dream machine. That you know."

"Then isn't it pointless, Jord Orlan, to destroy what they build?"

"It is not pointless because it is the Law. You are absurd to argue. Come now. Tell me about the location. I shall organize a group. We will smash the project completely."

"No," she said, smiling. "That would spoil my game. I am beginning to find it amusing. Leesa reserves that pleasure for herself, thank you."

"I can make that an order."

"And I shall disobey it and you can thrust me out of this world and perhaps never find the project."

He thought for a few moments. "It would be better were we to do it, a group of us. Then we should dream-kill the dream creatures with the greatest skills so as to lessen the danger of a new project for many years."

"No!" she said sharply. Then her eyes widened with surprise at the force of her own objection. She raised her fingertips to her lips.

"Now I understand," Jord Orlan said comfortably. "You find one of the dream creatures amusing, and you do not wish your sport to be denied you. Very well, then, but make certain that the destruction is complete. Report back to me."

As she reached the doorway he spoke to her again. She turned and waited. He said, "Within the next few days, my dear, Ryd Talleth will seek you out. I have ordered him to. He is the one most inclined to favor you—but he will need encouragement."

"He is a weak fool," she said hotly. "Do you not remember your promise, Jord Orlan? If I did as you asked, you would not force me into any such———"

"No one is forcing you. It is merely a suggestion," he said.

She walked away without answering him. She was restless. She walked down to the corridor lined with the small rooms for games. She stood in the doorway of one of them. Three women, so young that their heads still bore the thinning shadow of their dusty hair, pursued a squat and agile old man who dodged with cat-quick reflexes. They shrieked with laughter. He wore a wide grin. She saw his game. He favored one and it was his purpose to allow her to make the capture, even though the others were quicker. At last she caught him, her hands fast on the shoulder piece of the toga. The others were disconsolate. As they filed out of the room, leaving the two alone, Leesa turned away also. Once again she touched her lips and she thought of a man's heavy hands, square and bronzed against the whiteness of a hospital bed.

The next few rooms were empty. The following room was one with light controls. A mixed group was performing a stylized dance. They had turned the lights to blood red. It was a slow dance, with measured pauses. She thought of joining, but she knew that in some inexplicable way, her entrance would set up a tension that would remove some of their pleasure.

Restlessness was in her like slow spreading rot. On the next level she heard the sound of the small ones crying. She went and looked at them. Always, before, she had found a small pleasure in watching their unformed movements. She looked at them and their faces were like so many identical ciphers—circles of emptiness, signifying nothing.

She rode up to where the tracks no longer moved. She went halfway up to the twenty-first level, then dropped and curled like a child. She covered her face with her hands and wept. She did not know why she was weeping.

ELEVEN

BARD LANE HEARD HIS NAME CALLED. HE TURNED TO see Major Tommy Leeber striding diagonally across the street from the mess hall to intercept him.

Major Leeber's smile sat a shade stiffly on his lips and his eyes were narrowed.

"I hope you have a minute, Dr. Lane."

"Not very much more than that, I'm afraid, Major. What seems to be the trouble?"

"According to the records, Dr. Lane, my loyalty check was tops. And my brain waves passed all Sharan's witch-doctor techniques. So what's with these two shadows I've picked up?" He jerked his thumb back over his shoulder toward the two guards who stood several paces behind him, obviously uncomfortable.

"Those men are assigned to you in accordance with new operating instructions, Major."

"If you think you can chase me out of here by making me so uncomfortable that——"

"Major, I don't care for your tone, and I can't say much for your powers of observation. Everyone with access to fabrication zones and lab areas is subject to the new orders. You will notice that I have a guard too. We are in a critical phase. If you start acting irrational, you'll be grabbed and held until you can be examined. Me too. As a matter of fact, you have it a bit easier than I do.

Part of my job is to watch the guard while he watches me. We're using this method as a defense against any . . . temporary insanity where Dr. Inly did not detect the susceptibility of the employee."

"Look, how do I get rid of these boys?"

"Leave the project area, Major."

Leeber knuckled his chin. "Look, Doc. I happen to know that you're not getting new help in here. So where do the extra guards come from?"

"Other occupational classifications."

"Which slows down the works plenty, doesn't it?"

"Yes, it does."

"Already you are in plenty of hot water because of being so far behind schedule, Dr. Lane. Doesn't delaying it further seem to be a funny thing to do right now?"

For a moment Bard wondered how his knuckles would feel against the dark military moustache, the full lips. It would be a pleasure to see Major Leeber on the seat of his pants in the street.

"You may report this new development to General Sachson, Major. You may tell him that if he cares to, he can reverse this security regulation of mine. But it will be made a matter of record. Then, if someone else should get as destructive as Kornal did, the blame will be in his lap."

"For my money, Doc, the old man won't be too upset. He has it figured that inside of sixty days there won't be anybody here but a survey and salvage outfit, making chalk marks on whatever is worth keeping."

"I don't think you should have said that, Major Leeber," Bard said in a low voice. "I don't think it was smart."

He watched Leeber carefully, saw the greased wheels turning over slickly. Leeber grinned in his most charming way. "Hell, Doc. Don't mind me. I'm being nasty because these two boys tailing me have fouled up an operation that was all briefed out."

"I don't expect loyalty from you, Leeber. Just a reasonable cooperation."

"Then I apologize. I'm all lined up with a little blond cookie who runs a computer in the chem lab. And all I could think of was these two boys looking over my shoulder."

"Then take her out of the area, Leeber. When you report back in at the gate they'll make you wait until guards can be assigned."

Leeber scuffed the dust with the edge of his shoe. "A noble suggestion, Doc. Will you join me for a quick one?"

"I can't spare the time, thanks."

"Okay, I guess I don't want these boys joining in on my date. Guess I better take her out of the area, eh?"

"Either that or there'll be four of you. Five, when you count the guard assigned to her. A female guard."

Leeber shrugged, gave a mock salute, and sauntered away.

Bard Lane went into the mess hall. He took one of the small tables against the wall where he could be alone. He was lifting the glass of tomato juice to his lips when he felt the familiar pressure against his mind. He made no attempt to fight it. He held the glass poised in mid-air, then raised it to his lips. The sensation in his mind made him remember the first science courses he had taken in college. A hot afternoon, when he stared into the microscope, delicately adjusting the binocular vision until the tiny creatures in the droplet of swamp water had seemed to leap up at him. There had been one with a fringe of long cilia. It had slowly enfolded a smaller, more globular organism, merging with it, digesting it as he watched. He had long remembered the silent, microscopic ferocity, the instinctive ruthlessness of that struggle.

And now his mind was slowly devoured while he sat calmly drinking the juice. He replaced the glass in the saucer. To the onlooker he was Dr. Bard Lane—the boss —the chief—the "old man." But he knew that as far as free will was concerned he had ceased to be Bard Lane.

The alien prescience was quickly interlaced through his engram structure, much as a bobbin might shuttle back and forth in a textile machine. He sensed the fingering of his thoughts.

His new familiarity with the reception of the thoughts of the alien made those thoughts as clear as though they had been softly whispered in his ear.

"No, Bard Lane. No. You and Sharan Inly have come to the wrong conclusion. We are not of this planet. This is not a clever device to trick you. We are friendly to your purpose. I am glad to see that you have taken the precautions that were suggested to you. Please make it very clear to all your trusted people that they must move quickly whenever there is the slightest doubt. Any faint peculiarity—any unexpected word or movement will be the basis on which to move. Delay may be fatal."

Bard made his thoughts as clear as he could by mentally thinking each word, mentally underlining each syllable. "How do we know you *are* friendly?"

"You can't know. There's no way of proving it to you. All I can say is that our ancestors of twelve thousand years ago are mutual. I told you about the Plan. The Plan is failing because the people in my world have forgotten the original purpose. One world—Marith—lives in barbaric savagery. Another—Ormazd—has found the key to the search for happiness on their planet. We are inbred and decadent. Your project is hope for mankind."

"What are your motives?"

There was a silence in his mind. "If I am to be honest with you, Bard Lane, I must mention boredom, the desire for change, the wish to do important things. And now there is another reason."

"What?"

Their sympathetic emotional structure had been so carefully interleafed that Bard Lane was disconcerted to feel the hot blush on his cheeks and neck. "I want to be able to meet Sharan face to face. I want to touch her hand with mine, not with the hand of someone whom I could inhabit."

The thought broke hurriedly to other matters. "I have wondered if there is any way that I can give you technical help. I do not understand the formulas behind the operation of your ship. All I know is that propulsion is dependent on alternating frames of temporal reference. That is the same formula that was used for our ships long, long ago. As I told you, six of them stand outside our world. I have discovered micro-book operation manuals, but they are beyond me. I could memorize wiring charts and control panels and then, using your hand, draw them for you."

"There are problems we haven't licked yet. You could try to do that."

"What should I look for?"

"The manner in which astrogation charts were coordinated with the time jump. Our astronomers and mathematical physicists believe, at this point, that once the jump is made, it will take weeks to make observations and reorient the ship. They are working on some method which will extend the time jump as a hypothetical line through space from the starting point to the new time frame. Then the coordinates of that hypothetical line, using opposed star clusters for reference points, would eliminate starting from scratch on orientation in the new position. Can you follow that?"

"Yes. I will see if I can find out how it was done in the past."

The guard stepped closer and took a startlingly firm grasp of Bard Lane's arm just above the elbow. His expression was respectful, but his grasp was like iron.

"Sir, you have been talking aloud to yourself."

The alien prescience slid off to a spectator's cubicle within Bard's mind.

Bard smiled up at the guard. "Glad you're alert, Robinson. I'm doing some practice dictation on an important letter I have to write after lunch."

Robinson looked uncertain. Bard put his napkin beside his plate. "I'll be glad to go along to Dr. Inly's office, Robinson, but——"

"I think maybe you better, sir. The order was pretty strict."

Heads turned as they walked out of the mess hall, the bruising grip still punishing Bard's arm. He heard the buzz of conversation as the door swung shut behind them. The sunlight was a blow from a fist of gilt. They went down the street toward Sharan's office.

And the alarm sirens began to shrill.

Bard ripped away from Robinson's grasp and lifted his long legs into a hard run toward the communications center seventy yards away. The sirens died into a moan as he burst through the door. The man at the master switchboard, gray-pale with strain, glanced at Bard, cut in a wall baffle onto the circuit and said, "From the ship, sir. Go ahead. It'll be picked up."

"Who is this?" Bard demanded.

The answering voice was metallic. "Shellwand. On the ship. We've just found a guard on G level, near the shielding, laid out cold, sir. We're trying to get everyone out of the ship, sir."

"Who did it?"

"We won't know, sir, until we—— It's beginning to tremble, sir! The whole——"

The diaphragm in the baffle began to pick up resonance and bray. The man at the master board cut it off. They all heard it then. Once heard, it could never be forgotten. Bard Lane had heard it many times.

It was like the low roll of muted thunder behind distant hills, combined with a thousand roaring male voices, singing a sustained note in discord.

It was the song of men who try to reach the stars. It was the resonating fury of fission, held just short of instantaneous detonation. At Hiroshima it had been one thunderous whip-crack of fate that brought a new age to man. Now the whip-crack was harnessed, controlled, directed, guided.

Bard Lane turned and dived from the room. His shoulder caught the flimsy door and knocked it spinning from the torn hinges. He did not feel the pain. He ran out into an open space and stood with his feet planted, fists clenched, shoulders back, staring toward the Beatty One.

The thunder noise grew louder. Blue-white flame licked out around the fins. Heat cracked against his face and he turned his eyes from the unbearable glare. As the vast sound grew even greater the Beatty One nuzzled upwards at the camouflage tent. It rose with painful slowness, with the ponderousness of some unthinkable prehistoric beast. It ripped up through the tent, slowly gaining speed, profiling the tent to its ogive nose, tearing the tent from the towers, slipping through it, igniting it with the fierce tail flame. Now the blue-white unbearable flame was twice as tall as the ship had been. It reached from tail to earth, as though the Beatty One balanced on it.

The base of one tower, softened by heat-lick, settled and the tower leaned slowly toward the north, not gathering speed in the fall, just slowly bending over to lie gently against the ground. The steel of the elevator frame was puddled at the base, but stood miraculously erect. A tiny figure toppled from the elevator platform, crisping to blackness before it neared the ground.

The white gouting stern of the Beatty One was now thrice as high as the towers still standing. The thunder was lifting up through octave after octave as the speed of the Beatty One increased. A great flap of burning fabric fluttered down. The rest of the fabric slid off and the silvery length of the ship, a mirror in the sun, was revealed. Even with the despair that filled his heart, the horror and the great shock of failure, Bard Lane felt and recognized the strong sense of awe at the sheer beauty of the ship.

A tiny figure toppled from the high open port. The ship had moved just enough off the perpendicular so that the toy figure came down, not spinning, motionless in the sun-hot air, toward the street of the village. It hit in the dust, bursting work clothes, rebounding eighteen inches before lying still, a jellied, grotesque thing. The hard roar changed to shrillness and the Beatty One winked high in the sun. High and higher. Vapor trail. And higher. Then slowly canting over, as he knew it would do without the 20 Mohs stability plates which had not yet been installed in the A-six jet flow. It made a bright white line against the impossible blue of the sky, an arc, a parabola, as neat as any inscribed on graph paper. A line up to a peak and a line down. The shrillness was a scream that tore at the inner ear. A line down to the earth. He saw the flare and guessed the distance at fifteen to twenty miles, due south. The scream still continued after the explosion flare had filled half the sky, then stopped abruptly. The air pushed hard against them, then the earth shook as though a truck were going by. At last came the gutteral crack-boom of the explosion. And silence. Brown cloud lifting in mushroom shape toward the blue sky. A bit of the vapor trail was still high in the sky, wavering off in the prevailing wind.

Bard Lane took two steps to the curbing, sat down and held his face in his hands. Nearby, a wooden building crackled as the flames bit into it. The project fire engines screamed to a stop, sirens ridiculous in comparison to the memory of the scream of the dying Beatty One—a mosquito trying to outshout an eagle. Somebody rested a steady hand on Bard Lane's shoulder. He looked up and saw the stolid, seamed face of Adamson. Tears had cut channels in the dust on his cheeks.

"Nick, I . . . I . . ."

Adamson's voice was gruff. "I'll take an emergency crew down and see what she did when she hit. If we're lucky, she'll be five miles from the village. Better go get on the radio, Bard, and give the word. Then I think you ought to make an announcement over the PA." Adamson walked solidly away.

He walked to his office. The guard had voluntarily given up his assignment. The project personnel stood in the street. Not large groups. Two or three or four. Low voices. Long silences. They glanced quickly at him and then away. He went through the outer office. Bess Reilly sat at her desk. She sat with her forehead against the top of her typewriter. Her bony shoulders shook but she made no sound.

After he advised Sachson and Washington by coded

radio, he obtained a clear circuit over the PA for every amplifier in the area.

He spoke slowly. "This is Lane. We don't know what happened. We may never know who or what was responsible. You will be wondering about your jobs. I doubt very much whether we will be given a second chance. By the day after tomorrow we'll have the checks ready for termination pay for most of you. Certain clerical, stock record, and lab employees will be retained for a time. A list of those who will be needed will be posted on the bulletin board tomorrow afternoon. One thing. Don't ever feel that because of what just happened, all of what we have done is wasted. We learned things. If we're not given a chance to use them, someone else will, sooner or later. They will learn from the mistakes we made. All employees will please proceed immediately to the time clocks and remove their time cards. Turn them in to Mr. Nolan. Mr. Nolan, after there has been time for all cards to be picked up, send someone to gather up the unclaimed ones. That's the only way, I'm afraid, that we'll ever learn who made the . . . first and last trip on the Beatty One. Dr. Inly, please report to my office. Benton, rope off the takeoff area, and advise me when the count is down to a one hour safety period. Those of you who lost personal possessions in the barracks fire, prepare the standard claim form. You can get forms and instructions from Miss Mees in the Accounting Office. Brainard, start your labor crews to work torch-cutting, for scrap, the tower that fell outside the radiation area. The club will be closed tonight. And . . . I don't know how to say this properly, but I want to thank every single individual for . . . devotion and loyalty beyond anything I ever experienced before. Thank you."

He released the switch and looked up. Sharan Inly was standing in the doorway. She walked to his desk. "You wanted to see me."

He grinned in a very tired way. "Thanks, Sharan."

"For what?"

"For being bright enough not to start commiserating

with me, telling me how sorry you are and how it wasn't my fault and all that."

She sat down, hung one denimed leg over the arm of the chair. "There isn't anything to say. Our good pal who calls himself Raul got to one of the group and fixed us. On the other side of the world somebody feels very, very good, I imagine."

"What are you going to do, Sharan?"

"They'll find another slot to put me in. Maybe I'll be back in the Pentagon, testing the Oedipus complexes of quartermaster second lieutenants. Something frightfully thrilling along that line. But now I have a hobby."

"Hobby?"

"Finding out how they worked that long-range hypnosis. There are a few people I can trust not to think I've lost my mind when I give them the story."

"But you won't be taking off immediately, I'm afraid. There'll be an investigation. We'll have the star parts. You and I and Adamson and Leeber and Kornal and a few of the others. Stick around, Dr. Inly. See the big three-ring circus. Hear the tigers howl for meat. Pay your money and see the seven wonders of the world."

A storm front was moving in from the north. The day was unexpectedly and unusually muggy. Extra chairs had been brought into General Sachson's conference room. Two bored girls sat at a small table near the windows, supplementing the recording devices with the aid of two stenotype machines. They had covered several yards of the white tape with the staggered letters. The door was closed against the reporters and photographers who waited in the corridor.

Bard Lane sat at the witness table. His armpits were sodden and he had a dry, stained taste in his mouth.

Senator Leedry was a dry wisp of a man, tiny and withered, but with a plump and arrogant little paunch. He smiled as he spoke. His baritone voice was alternately scalpel, cutting torch, and caress.

"I appreciate, Dr. Lane, your attempts to explain technical data in a manner that we poor laymen can understand. Believe me, we *appreciate* it. But I guess we're not as bright as you imagine. At least, I'm not. Now, if it isn't too much trouble, would you explain once again to us, your *theory* about the accident."

"The A-six uses what they call, in Army slang, 'soft' radiation. The shielding also acts as an inhibitor. When actuated, the pellets are fed down to the CM chamber for combustion. The CM chamber utilizes the principles of the old shaped charge to achieve thrust. The controls had not been installed for the A-six drive. There is no possibility of an accidental transfer of pellets to the drive chamber."

The Secretary of War, Logan Brightling, cleared his throat to interrupt. Cartoons depicted him perfectly as a hairless Kodiak bear wearing a wing collar. "Why was the Beatty One equipped with the hot stuff for the A-six drive before the controls were installed?"

"In spite of the inhibitors, the pellets generate appreciable heat. The Beatty One had an efficient method of utilizing this heat for self-contained power. To use that power for the necessary welding and structural work was more efficient than attempting to bring outside power to the ship. You could say that once we had the internal power source working, the Beatty One was helping to build herself. To continue, I have explained that I do not feel that it could have been an accident. The wall chart shows a schematic cross section." Bard Lane walked over to the chart. "A man could enter here. It is the normal inspection procedure to check the shielding at regular intervals and take a careful count of all escaping radiation to determine whether or not it is well within safety limits. From this passage a man can work his way completely around the shielding and the drive chamber. At this point is a port that can only be used when the storage section contains no pellets. Beyond the port the radiation will kill a man in approximately twelve minutes. Once through that port it would take a person not more than three minutes to manually dislodge the pellets from their niches in the conveyor and drop them down onto the plate above the drive chamber. In a few minutes more the person could clamber down there, activate the motor on the plate and let the pellets drop into the drive chamber itself. Without the required inhibition, the CM would be instantaneously achieved and the ship would take off. Inspection of the area where the Beatty One stood has shown us that there is more residual radiation than would normally be expected. Thus we assume that the drive chamber was fed with more pellets than would normally have been carried there at one time by the conveyor, and thus we can assume that it was not an accidental actuation of the conveyor itself."

Leedry pursed his dry lips. "Then, Dr. Lane, you would have us believe that someone went into that . . . that searing hell of radiation and sabotaged the ship?"

Bard returned to his chair. "I can see no other answer. After five seconds by the open port to the storage section, there would be not the slightest hope of living more than twenty minutes no matter what medical attention was given. The person sacrificed his life. There were twelve technicians on the ship at the time, along with twelve guards watching them under a new security bulletin I issued four days before the accident. Evidently the saboteur overpowered his guard. The elevator operator and two laborers too close to the ship perished, bringing the total death toll in the takeoff to twenty-seven. A large section of the burning camouflage cover fell on a typist from the accounting office. She died yesterday of her burns. So the total is twenty-eight."

General Sachson went over to Leedry, bent down and whispered in his ear. Leedry did not change expression. He said, "Dr. Lane, would you please move over to the other table for a few minutes. Dr. Inly, will you please come forward."

Leedry let the seconds mount up. Sharan concealed the thud of her pulse, the sick nervousness that gave her mouth a metallic taste.

"Dr. Inly, you have previously testified as to your du-

ies and the operating regulations which have covered
hose duties. As I understand your regulations, once you
have committed any project employee for detailed observation, the minimum length of time in hospital is seven
days. Yet, according to your records, we find that Dr.
Lane was sent in for observation and released after only
three days. I trust you have some explanation of this deviation from your stated regulations."

There was a buzz of conversation in the room. The
chairman of the investigating committee rapped for order.

Sharan bit her lip.

"Come, Dr. Inly. Surely you know why you ordered
Dr. Lane's release!"

"I discovered that . . . the evidence on which I had
committed Dr. Lane was not what . . . I had first
thought."

"Is it true that you have been very friendly with Dr.
Lane? Is it not true that you have often been alone together? Is it not true that there was a very strong rumor
among the project employees that your relationship was
—shall we say—a bit closer than a normal professional
relationship would indicate?" Leedry leaned forward in
his chair, as intent as a questing hawk.

"I resent your implication, Senator."

"Merely answer the questions, Dr. Inly."

"Dr. Lane is my very good friend. Nothing more. We
were often together and we often discussed what courses
of action would be best for the project."

"Indeed?" Leedry asked.

Bard stood up. "Senator, I consider this line of investigation as wholesome as scribbling on a lavatory wall."

"You're out of order!" the chairman snapped. "Sit
down, please."

"Take the stand again, Dr. Lane," Leedry said. "We
will need you again in a few moments, Dr. Inly."

Bard took the stand. Leedry again waited for his fellow
committee members to stop their whispers. "Dr. Inly is
quite attractive, don't you think?" he asked Bard in a jo-
vial manner.

"She is a competent psycholgist," Bard said.

"Ah, undoubtedly. Now then, Dr. Lane. Yesterday we took testimony from one of the hospital supervisors. Can you explain how it was that you were seen in the hospital making love to a young nurse named Anderson?"

"May I ask what you are trying to prove?" Bard asked. His voice was low.

"I'll be glad to tell you, Dr. Lane. I can best tell you by asking you one more question. Dr. Lane, you are quite a famous man, you know. You are quite young for the enormous responsibilities which were given you. You have spent a trifle more than one billion dollars of the taxpayers' money. Money that came from a great number of little people who work hard for a living. Surely you felt the weight of that responsibility. Now answer me this question, Dr. Lane. During the period of time since you permitted one William Kornal to return to his duties after having smashed key control equipment, have you at any time sincerely felt that you are and have been unsuited for the responsibilities which were given you?"

Bard Lane doubled his big brown fists. He glanced at Sharan Inly and saw that her eyes were misty. "Yes, I have."

"And yet you did not ask to be relieved?"

"No, sir."

"Dismissed. Wait in the anteroom. Please take the stand, Major Leeber. I understand that you have been in the position of an observer ever since the Kornal incident."

"That is correct." Major Leeber sat very straight in his chair. Each bit of brass on his uniform was a tiny golden mirror. His voice had lost the lazy tone. It was crisp. His mouth was a firm line.

"Will you give us your opinion of the quality of Dr Lane's management?"

"I can best do that by giving the committee a verbatim quote from a report I sent to General Sachson, my commanding officer, three days before the 'accident' occurred I am quoting paragraph three of my report. 'It appear that Dr. Lane is best suited to perform supervised technical work in the research field and that he has neither the temperament nor the training for administrative work that is required of the head of a project such as this one. The informality here is indicative of a lack of discipline. Dr. Lane goes to ridiculous lengths in his new security regulations, detailed above, yet permits fraternization between high-level personnel and CAF-two typists on the clerical staff. The undersigned officer strongly recommends that every attempt be made to bring this situation to the attention of those persons in Washington who are in a position to direct a full scale investigation of the project.'"

Leedry turned to Sachson. "General, don't bother taking the stand. Just tell us what you did with the major's report."

"I endorsed it, stating my approval of Leeber's conclusions and sent it by courier officer through the Chief of Ordnance to the Commanding General, Armed Forces. I assumed that it would be taken up with the Secretary of Defense."

The Secretary of Defense rumbled, "It was on my desk for my personal attention when the flash came that the Beatty One had taken off prematurely. I compliment the General and Major Leeber on their handling of this matter. I shall see that it is made a matter of record for their two-oh-one files."

Sharan Inly laughed. The sound was out of place in the room. The laugh was as chill as the tinkling of crystal. "Gentlemen, you amuse me. The Army has resented Project Tempo from the beginning. The Army feels that space travel attempts are absurd unless carried on in an atmosphere of company formations, service ribbons and seventh endorsements. Dr. Lane is caught in the middle and he'll be disgraced. The sad truth is that he has more integrity in his little finger than Major Leeber is even capable of visualizing." She turned to Leeber and said mildly, "You really are a rather despicable little man, you know. Gentlemen, this whole affair makes me sick at heart and rather close to being ill in quite another manner. I am leaving and you can cite me for contempt or restrain me physically. I imagine the latter will be more your style. So nice to have known you."

She brushed by the sergeant at arms at the door. It closed gently behind her.

"Let her go," Leedry said. "I rather imagine that she'll have a long, long wait before Civil Service is able to place her in another government position. And she just told us all we need to know. Her infatuation with Lane, and the effect of that infatuation on her judgment is now a matter of record. I suggest that we consider arriving at a conclusion. My personal opinion is that Project Tempo failed due to the gross negligence and mental instability of Dr. Bard Lane. We should clear out the witnesses and poll the committee."

General Sachson, as he stood up, said, "If I could have the privilege of making one comment, Senator."

"Of course, General," Leedry said warmly.

"You will find in my record that two years ago when Project Tempo was being considered, I read the survey reports and filed a negative opinion. That girl—I should say Dr. Inly—inferred that the military has attempted to block Project Tempo. I wish to deny that allegation. I am a soldier. I follow orders. Once Project Tempo was approved, I gave it my wholehearted cooperation. The minutes of my staff meetings in connection with Tempo are available as proof of this cooperation.

"However, in all honesty, I must confess that from the beginning I considered Tempo to be a wild scheme. I believe that with persistence, with the application of discipline and effort, we will succeed in conquering space in accordance with the plan outlined by General Roamer sixteen years ago. First we must beef up our moon base. The moon is the stepping stone to Mars and Venus. Gentlemen, it is sound military thought to consolidate your own area before advancing further. Project Tempo put the cart several miles ahead of the horse. The old ways are the best. The known methods are tried, and they will be true.

"Is this time-jump theory something you can see, feel, hold on to? No. It is a theory. I personally do not believe that there is any variation. I think time is a constant throughout all the galaxies and all the universe. Lane was a dreamer. I am a doer. You know my record. I do not want this fiasco to make you turn your backs on space flight. We need a vastly augmented moon base. From a moon base we can look down the throat of Pan-Asia. We must reinforce that base, and not dissipate our efforts in humoring the more lunatic fringe of our nation's physicists. Thank you, gentlemen."

Leedry led the round of polite but enthusiastic applause. Major Leeber rose quickly to his feet and clapped with the rest.

TWELVE

FOR AN UNCOUNTED NUMBER OF DAYS, RAUL KINSON SAT in one of the rooms of learning, alone, many levels above the rest of the Watchers. Infrequently he went down to pick at the food on one of the trays. Once Leesa found him. He did not look at her, or hear what she said. He was vaguely aware of her presence and felt a mild distant relief when she went away.

Over and over and over again he saw, as he had seen it through Bard Lane's eyes, the roaring ruin of the Beatty One, the ruin of his hopes, the clear cue to treachery. He wanted Leesa's throat between his fingers, yet knew that he could not kill her.

He did not dream. He did not wish to project himself back to Earth. He had been ashamed of the Watchers before. This was a new shame, more intense than ever before. And slowly he came back to life. Hour by hour. On Earth there had been one ship. Here there were six. Would a man die outside the building? If a man could live, could he find his way into one of the six ships . . .

He knew where the door was. If he died outside the building, it did not matter.

He went down to the lowest level, hurried by the throb of the power rooms, glancing often over his shoulder. He made certain that he was not followed. The rooms that lined the corridor leading to the door contained things that the others no longer understood. Odd garments. Tools. Undisturbed for centuries.

At last he came to the door. The top of it was on a level with his eyes. Two spoked wheels projected from the door itself. He touched one. It turned easily. He spun it hard. It spun without sound, stopped with a soft click. He did the same with the other one. He glanced back up the corridor, then grasped both wheels. His breath came deep and hard and excitement fluttered along his spine. He pulled slowly. The door opened. He knew of wind and coldness, but always he had felt them in an alien body and now he knew that such sensations had been muted. The wind was a dull knife scraping his flesh and sand, heaped against the door, trickled in onto the corridor floor. He knew that he could not stand such cold. The sand prevented him from closing the door again. He dropped to his knees and shoveled the sand back out with his hands. At last he could close the door. As he leaned against it he began to stop shaking as the warmth seeped back into his body. It seemed incredible that beyond the door there was not another corridor, equally warm.

He found the garments in the third room. They were metallic, dark green. The inner lining was soft. He found a large one, put it on awkwardly. It felt strange against his legs, heavy. The fastening was difficult until he discovered that the two strips of metal down the front would cling together firmly of their own accord.

Thus clad against the cold, it was only as he returned to the door the second time that he thought of a more obvious danger. When shut the door would remain closed until he pushed against it from the outside. But if Jord

Orlan or any one of the old ones should be following him, should come and spin the wheels——

"Raul!" she said, close behind him. It startled him badly. He turned and stared at Leesa, then turned his back to her.

"Raul, you must listen to me. You must!"

"There is nothing you can say to me."

"I know what you think of me. I betrayed you, Raul. I gave you my word and betrayed you. You know that I smashed that ship." She laughed in a strange and brittle way. "But you see, I didn't realize that I was betraying myself too."

He did not turn. He stood stolidly, staring at the burnished metal of the door.

"I have dreamed many times, Raul, trying to find him. I have found Sharan Inly. I told her what I had done. She hated me, Raul. And after a long time I made her understand. She is . . . kind, Raul. But she cannot find him. No one knows where he has gone. And I must find him and tell him . . . why I did that to him."

Behind him he heard an odd sound. A small sound. He turned. She had dropped to her knees, and sat on her heels, shoulders slumped, face in her hands.

"Never before have I seen you weep, Leesa."

"Help me find him, Raul. Please help me."

"I want you to find him, Leesa. I want you to see, in his mind, precisely what you did to him."

"I know what I did to him. I was in his mind once, Raul, after it happened," she said, lifting her tear-tracked face. "It was . . . horrid."

"How can that be, Leesa? Remember? They are only dream creatures. They don't exist. The machines are clever. The dream machines manufactured Bard Lane for our special amusement."

"Don't. Please don't."

"Don't tell me, my sister, that you have come to believe those creatures exist," he said mockingly. "What could have changed your mind?"

Her eyes were grave on his. There was an odd dignity

about her. "I cannot think it out the way you do. I was in his mind. I know his thoughts, his memories and his dreams. I know him better than I know myself. It is just that I cannot go on living in a universe where he does not exist. And if he exists, then all the others do. You have been right. All the others have been wrong, as wrong as I have been."

"I should trust you now?"

"Is there any reason for distrusting me . . . now?"

He took her hands and lifted her to her feet, and he smiled. "I shall trust you again. If you help me, maybe we can find him again. I know how you feel, Leesa, because I cannot . . . stop thinking, remembering. She was . . ."

"Sharan Inly?"

He turned away from her. "Yes, and a cruel trap for both of us, Leesa."

"How can I help you?"

"I am going out to the ships. I am going to try to board one. I have learned some of the operating instructions. Our lifetimes will be long over before Earth builds another ship like the one you destroyed. Those ships out there have the same principle. I shall board one and I shall take it to Earth."

Her eyes grew wide, shocked. "But . . ."

"It may be too cold out there. I may die. There may not be enough oxygen left on this planet. If I fail, you will go in that second room. Select a tool that cuts cables. Take it up to the dream cases by stealth. Start with the unused cases. Cut the cables on every one. Every one. Do you understand?"

"Then I will never find him."

"That would be a good thing. I do not want to go to Sharan Inly in some other body. I want to go and touch her with this hand, look at her with these eyes. Nothing else is any good."

"One of those ships . . . after so many years . . . it is incredible, Raul."

"I've had the door open. I think I can live out there. Help me. Wait for me here. I must be able to get back in side. If anyone should come, you must keep them from touching those wheels on the door. Do you understand?"

"Yes."

He went to the door and pulled it open. He saw her shrink away from the shrill wind. He lowered his head and plunged out. She pushed the door shut. He stood for a moment, turning his back to the wind, finding out if he could breathe the air. He had to breathe fast and deep. The cold bit into his bones and the sand scoured the naked backs of his hands and his cheeks. He turned and squinted across the dim plain toward the six ships. With the position determined, he walked toward them, leaning into the wind, shielding his eyes with his hand, holding the other hand in his armpit for warmth. As the unprotected hand began to grow numb, he changed hands. He looked again and saw that his hundred steps had carried him off to the left. He corrected his direction and continued on. A hundred steps more. The ships seemed no closer. The next time he looked they were closer. And then, panting with the exertion, he saw new details of their construction. He turned his back to the wind and cried out as he saw his known world far behind him. Taller than the ships, yet dwarfed by the ragged hills behind it, it reached white levels up toward the purpled sky. Blank featureless walls, each level recessed a bit, reaching up to a dizzy height above him.

He fought the desire to return. He went on. Behind him, the wind erased his tracks. The ships grew larger. Their fluted sterns rested on the sand. One of them was canted at a slight angle. Never had he realized their true size, nor their distance from each other. The last hundred feet was the easiest because the nearest ship cut the force of the harsh, steady wind. The sand was piled high in long sharp ridges extending out on either side of the ship. Above him, the bulge of the ship was a dizzy overhang. The surface, though still of shining metal, was pitted and scarred and worn. And there was no way to get into the ship. No way at all. He circled it, almost weeping in frustration. Shining and unclimbable metal. He steadied himself with one hand against it as he clambered awkwardly over the drifts. Both

hands were so numb that he could not feel the texture of
the metal against his fingers. He made two complete cir-
cuits of the ship. Across the plain the tall white world
seemed to watch with silent amusement.

He tripped and fell heavily. His face struck against the
side of the ship, half stunning him. He lay, trying to sum-
mon up the energy he would need to get back to his feet.
The ship was inches from his eyes. He tensed. An angular
crack showed in the metal, too straight to be accidental.
He sat with spread legs, like a child in a sand pile, and dug
with hands that were like clubs. The crack grew, turned
into the right angle of what could be a square port. He
began to laugh as he dug, chuckling deep in his throat,
over the wind-scream.

He stopped digging and patted the ship affectionately,
called it words of endearment. And now he felt much
warmer. Pleasantly warm.

He fumbled up onto his feet with drunken dignity.
Pretty ship. Take him to Earth. See Sharan.

Raul turned. No need to go to Earth after all. There was
Sharan, standing there, smiling. She didn't mind the wind.
She was warm too. He advanced toward her and she
backed away, teasingly. His feet made no tracks in the
sand.

"Sharan!" he bawled hoarsely, his voice lost in the constant wind-shriek. "Sharan!" He lifted his unfeeling legs in
a stumbling run. She was still elusive, backing toward the
white warm world he had left. He hoped Leesa was watching, so that she could see Sharan too. Now Sharan was
gone. He couldn't find her. He ran on and tripped and fell
headlong. He was far too comfortable to get up. Too
warm. The sand piled quickly up along his left side, and at
last spilled across the back of his neck with a gentle touch
that was like a caress.

THIRTEEN

SHARAN INLY LOOKED WITH DISTASTE AT THE NARROW street. The man from the agency pulled up at the curb and stopped. It was dusk and neon was beginning to flicker.

The agency man pointed toward the place called Joe's Alibi.

"He'll be in there, miss. Want me to go yank him out? It's no place for a girl, and he won't be in any shape to come willingly."

"I'll go in," she said.

"I better come with you then. You'll need help with him."

"If you wish," she said.

The agency man looked at the grubby children nearby, carefully locked the car before crossing the street with her.

They heard hoarse laughter as they crossed the sidewalk. The laughter and the rumble of conversation stopped as Sharan pushed the screen open and walked in. She walked into the room and then turned to the agency man.

"He's not here," she said with sinking heart.

"Take a second look, miss," he said.

She looked at the man at the table. His chair was tilted back against the wall. His chin was on his chest and he was asleep. His gaunt gray face was stubbled with beard and his open collar was soiled.

Sharan went quickly to the table. "Bard!" she cried softly. "Bard!"

"That his name?" the bartender said in the silence. "We call him the perfessor. He's what you might call a mascot around here. You want him woke up?"

The heavy-shouldered bartender came around the corner of the bar, tilted Bard's chair forward, caught him on the front of the stained suit, lifted him effortlessly and slapped his cheek with a full arm swing. It resounded like a pistol shot.

"Take it easy, friend," the agency man said softly.

Bard opened his eyes owlishly. "Now listen to his act," the bartender said. "Perfessor! Can you hear me, Perfessor? Tell us about them Martians."

In a hollow, whisky-hoarse tone, Bard said, "They come to us from a distant planet and take over our souls. They fill our minds with evil and lead us to dark deeds. You never know when they are coming. No one ever knows. We should be on guard."

"Cute, ain't he?" the bartender said, grinning.

Sharan curled her fingers and took a half step toward the bartender. "Get away from him," she whispered.

"Sure, lady. Sure thing. No harm intended."

Bard found her with his eyes. He frowned. "What do you want?"

"Come with me, Bard."

"I like it here. Sorry," he mumbled.

The agency man stepped around her. He caught Bard's wrist, brought it around and up into the small of Bard's back. Bard made feeble struggles. The agency man marched him to the door as Sharan followed.

"Take good care of the perfessor, sweetheart," one of the customers said. Sharan flushed. The room was once again filled with laughter.

She unlocked the car and the agency man edged Bard in onto the seat. As soon as Bard was sitting, he fell asleep again. He was between them as the agency man started the car. "Smells a little strong, don't he?" the agency man said.

Sharan didn't answer. The rooming house was in the next block. It was a scabrous building, full of the memories of evil, of the wry ghosts of orgy.

"Second floor front," the agency man said. He woke Bard up. Bard Lane seemed dazed. There was no more protest in him. Sharan followed them up the stairs, the agency man supporting Bard with an arm around his waist. The door was unlocked. The room was tiny, shabby, and the hall was sour and dim.

"You want I should stay and help you, lady?" the man asked.

"Thank you. I'll take it from here on," she said. "And thank you."

"All in the day's work. Be careful. Some of them go a little nutty when you start to wring them out."

He had collapsed on the narrow bed. He snored. She unlocked the door behind her and took the key. In an hour she was back with a complete set of new clothes that would fit him. She turned on the single light, cleaned up some of the litter in the room. The bath was across the hall. No shower. Just a tub.

His shoes were cracked and broken things that could have come from a trash barrel. He wore no socks. His ankles were grubby. She laid out his shaving things, the new clothes, in the bathroom.

Then came the nightmare of waking him, of seeing the eyes open vague in the gray face. He no longer seemed to know her. She supported more than half his weight getting him across the hall. He could not help himself. He sat on the stool with his back against the wall and let himself be undressed, like a child. Getting him into the tub was a major engineering project, and then she had to wait until the cold water revived him enough so that she could be sure he did not drown. She went out and brought back a quart of hot coffee. He drank it and looked at her with a bit more comprehension.

"Bard! Listen to me. Clean up and get dressed."

"Sure, sure," he mumbled.

From time to time she went back to the bathroom door and listened. She heard him splashing, moving around. Later she heard the scrape of a razor. She bundled his old clothes in the plastex wrapper that had been around the new clothes.

At last he came slowly into the room. He sat down quickly, cupped trembling hands over his eyes. "How do you feel?" she asked.

"Rotten, Sharan."

"There's some coffee beside you. Better have some." Even with the container held in both hands, some of the hot coffee spilled out onto the back of his hand.

"You didn't find a very good answer, did you?" she said.

"Is any answer a good one?"

"Giving up isn't a good answer."

"Please. Spare me the violin music. I was discarded. It seemed necessary to act the part."

"Everybody has a streak of martyr, Bard."

He stared at her. His eyes were hollow, lifeless. "They fixed me good. They tied the can to me, baby. No lab in the country would touch me. You know that. I had some money saved. I was going to show everybody. I interviewed some accident victims—the ones where I suspected Raul and his gang had a part in it. I took a tape recorder. Know the most common expression? 'I don't know what came over me,' they said. I tried to get a newspaper interested. They talked very pleasantly while they sent for the little men with the nets."

"I read about it, Bard," she said softly.

"Good article, wasn't it? Funny as hell."

"You haven't been in the ne. .r a month. The public has a short memory. They've forgotten you."

"That's a comfort."

"Feel better now?"

He stared at her. "Dr. Inly, the patient refuses treatment. Why don't you go exercise a few prefrontal lobes or something?"

She smiled at him. "Don't be childish. Finish the coffee. We're going to get you a haircut and a steak—in that order."

His smile was mild acid. "And why do I merit all this attention?"

"Because you are needed. Don't be defensive, Bard. Just do as I say. I'll explain later."

Dusk was over the city and they were in an oak booth

at the back of a quiet restaurant. His eyes were brighter and some of the shakiness had gone out of his hands. He pushed his coffee cup aside, lit her cigarette and his own. "Now it's time to talk, Sharan."

"We'll talk about a mistaken premise, Bard. We assumed that a hypnotic device operated from the other side of this world destroyed the Beatty One. After they delicately told me that I was all through and that I'd be called if there was a vacancy for anyone with my rating, I was ... contacted again. With the Beatty One gone, there didn't seem to be much point in it. I jeered at their fantasy of an alien world. I jeered at our friend, Raul, and at his sister. It took them a long time. I brought Lurdorff in on it. He's too egocentric to ever doubt his own sanity. And now he believes, too. They're what they say they are."

He stared at her without expression. "Go on."

"Everything he told us appeared to be true. It was the girl who destroyed the ship. She took over the A-six technician named Machielson. She had him overpower the guard. The rest of it went just the way you guessed. Bard, do you remember the time I told you that I wished I could fall in love with you?"

"I remember."

"Someone else did. The sister. She found out too late. She thought we were figments of her dreams. Now she, like Raul, is convinced that we are reality. The logical processes of most women are rather odd. She and her brother have been helping me look for you. I explained about investigation agencies and how expensive they were. The next day a man stopped me in the street and gave me all of the money out of his wallet and walked on. A second and a third man did the same. That's the way Raul fixed the money angle. And now we've found you."

Bard stubbed out his cigarette. He laughed softly. "Sort of a long range affair, isn't it? Raul identified their planet as being near Alpha Centauri. If he gave me a picture of what is actually their world, my lady love has a bald and gleaming skull, the body of a twelve year old child. I can hardly wait."

"Don't make a joke out of it, Bard!" she said with some heat. "We need you. If we're ever going to live up to the promise that we had in the Beatty One, you have to help us."

"I see. Raul gets one billion people to each hand us a dollar and then we start from scratch."

She stood up quickly and stubbed out her cigarette. "All right, Bard. I thought you might want to help. I'm sorry. I was wrong. It was good to see you again. Good luck." She turned away.

"Come back and sit down, Sharan. I'm sorry."

She hesitated, came back. "Then listen. Of all men on this planet, you have the best overall grasp of the problems involved in the actual utilization of Beatty's formulas. Some forgotten man on Raul's planet perfected those formulas roughly thirteen thousand years before Beatty did. Raul has gotten to the ships he told you about. He nearly died in the attempt. When he was gone too long the first time, Leesa went out after him and managed to get him back before he froze to death. He has been in one of the ships a dozen times. He thinks that it is still in working condition. He has activated certain parts of it—the air supply, internal heating. But as far as the controls are concerned, you are the only one who can help. He is baffled."

"How can I help?"

"We discussed that. He can use your hand to draw, from memory, the exact position of every knob and switch, along with a translation of the symbols that appear on them. If the principle is the same, which he is almost certain that it is, then you should be able to figure out the most logical purpose of each control."

"But . . . look, Sharan, the odds against my being right. They're tremendous. And the smallest mistake will leave him lost in space, or aflame on the takeoff. Or suppose he does find us. Suppose he barrels into our atmosphere at ten thousand miles per second and makes his landing in Central Park or the Chicago Loop district?"

"He's willing to take the chance."

She let him think without interruption. He drew aimless lines on the tablecloth with his thumbnail. "What would be gained?"

"What would the Beatty One have gained? And you do read the papers, don't you? Mysterious crash of stratoliner. Father slays family of six. Bank embezzler throws two millions into Lake Erie. Novelist's girlfriend buried alive. Auto charges noon crowds on busy street corner. We've always considered that sort of thing inexplicable, Bard. We've made big talk about irrational spells, about temporary insanity, about the way the human mind is prone to go off balance without warning. Isn't that sort of thing worth stopping, even at a billion to one chance? Religions have been born out of the fantasies the Watchers have planted in the minds of men. Wars have been started for the sake of amusing those who have considered us to be merely images given the appearance of reality by a strange machine."

Again the silence. He smiled. "How do we start?"

"We've worked out a coordinated time system. Their 'days' are longer than ours. We'll have to go to my place. They expect me to bring you there so that contact can be made. It is quicker than searching each time. We have an hour before we have to get there."

She had a hotel suite. Bedroom and sitting room. Physically there were two people in the room. Mentally there were four. Bard sat in a deep chair, the floor lamp shining down on the pad he held against his knee. Sharan stood by the window.

Through Bard's lips, Raul said, "We'll have to make this a four-way discussion, and so all thoughts will have to be vocalized. How will we make identification?"

Sharan said, "This is Leesa speaking. Raul, when you or I speak, we'll hold up the right hand. That should serve."

It was agreed. Bard felt the uncanny lifting of his right hand without his own conscious volition. "In Dr. Lane's mind, Sharan and Leesa, I still find considerable doubt.

He seems willing to go along with us, but he is still skeptical." The hand dropped.

Bard said, "I can't help it. And I admit to certain animosity, too. Leesa, as I understand it, ruined Project Tempo."

Sharan lifted her right hand. "Only because I didn't understand, then. Believe me, Bard. Please. You have to believe me. You see, I——"

Bard's right hand lifted and Raul said, "Leesa, we haven't time for that sort of thing. Don't interrupt for a moment. I want to draw the instrument panel for Dr. Lane."

Bard Lane felt the pressure that forced him further back from the threshold of volition. His hand grasped the pencil. Quickly a drawing of an old instrument panel began to take shape. Across the top were what appeared to be ten square dials. Each one was calibrated vertically, with a zero at the middle, plus values above, minus values below the zero point. The indicator was a straight line across the dial resting on the zero point. Below each dial were what appeared to be two push buttons, one above the other. Raul murmured, "This is the part that I cannot understand. I have figured out the rest of the controls. The simplest one is directional. A tiny replica of the ship is mounted on a rod at the end of a universal joint. The ship can be turned manually. From what I have gathered from the instruction manuals, the replica is turned to the desired position. The ship itself follows suit, and as it does so, the replica slowly moves back to the neutral position. Above the ten dials is a three-dimensional screen. Once a planet is approached, both planet and ship show on the screen. As the ship gets closer to the surface, the scale becomes smaller so that actual terrain details appear. Landing consists of setting the ship image gently against the image of the planet surface. Such maneuvering is apparently on the same basis as the Beatty One. But there is no hand control for it. There are diaphragms to strap on either side of the larynx and velocity is achieved through the intensity with which a certain vowel is uttered. I tested that portion of the ship by making the vowel sound as softly as I could. The ship trembled. I imagine that the purpose is to enable the pilot to control the ship even when pressure keeps him from lifting a finger. I feel capable of taking the ship up and landing it again. But unless I can understand the ten dials below the three-dimensional screen, it is obvious that no extended voyage can be made."

The pressure faded. Bard said, "Have you tried to discover the wiring details behind the dials?"

"Yes. I cannot understand it. And it is so complicated that by memorizing one portion at a time and transmitting that portion to you, I feel that it would take at least one of your years before it would be complete, and then I would have no real assurance that it was entirely accurate."

"Plus and minus values, eh? How good is your translation of the figures? Is your math equivalent to ours?"

"No. Your interval is ten. Ours is nine. The roughest possible comparison would be to say that your value for twenty is the second digit in our third series."

"Then the nine plus and nine minus values above and below the zero cover a full simple series. I am always wary of snap judgments, but those dials remind me, unmistakably, of the answer column in any computing device. With ten dials and only plus values alone, you could arrive at our equivalent of one billion. Adding in the minus values, you can achieve a really tremendous series of values. The available numbers could be computed as one billion multiplied by nine hundred and ninety-nine million, nine hundred and ninety-nine thousand, nine hundred and ninety-nine. Navigation always assumes known coordinates. Assume, for a moment, that the basic future-past relationship is expressed as plus and minus. Assume further that utilizing the varying frames of temporal reference, it is necessary to cross, at the very most, ten time lines to arrive at the most distant star—the star that, from your position, is equidistant no matter in which direction you start out. Now, for any nearer star, there will be a preferred route. There will be an assumed direction. You will intersect the frames of reference at an assumed point. Thus, your controls should be so set as to take advantage, at the proper fractional part of a second, of your plus-minus, or, more accurately, your future-past distortions. This would mean an index number, starting from your position, for each star—not a fixed index number, but a number which, adjusted by a formula to allow for orbital movement and galactic movement, will give you the setting for the controls. One of the unknowns to fit into the equation before using it is your present value for time on your planet. No. Wait a minute. If I were designing the controls I would use a radiation timing device for accuracy, and have the controls work the formula themselves so that the standard star reference number could always be used."

"It will have to be that way. It has been centuries since we have maintained any record of elapsed time."

"The buttons under the dials should be the setting device. The upper button should, with each time you push it, lift your indicator one plus notch. The lower button should drop it, one notch at a time, into the minus values. The final number, placed on the dials, should take you across space to the star for that specific setting. It would be the simplest possible type of control which could be used with the Beatty formulas—far simpler than the one on which we were working. But to use it, you must find somewhere, probably on the ship, a manual which will give you a listing of the values for the stars."

Bard Lane felt the excitement in Raul Kinson's thoughts. "A long time ago. Three of your years. Possibly more. I found books printed on thin metallic plates. They did not mean anything to me. Long bi-colored numbers. They were awkward to read compared with the microbooks. I remember the cover design—a stylized pattern of a star and planet system."

"That could be what you need. But let me make one thing clear. If I'm correct about the controls, and if you should use the wrong setting, you will, in all probability, never be able to find either Earth or your home planet again. You could spend forty lifetimes searching, with the same chance of finding either as of finding two specific motes of dust in the atmosphere of this planet. Make certain that you are quite willing to take the risk."

Leesa said softly, "Quite willing, Bard."

"Then find these books again. Study the numbers. See if they will fit the dials. See if you can determine our index number beyond doubt. And then contact me again."

Pressure on his mind faded quickly. Before it was entirely gone, Bard caught the faint thought: "This dream is ending."

The two of them were alone in the room. Sharan said softly, "Can he do it? Can he come here?"

He stood up and walked over to the windows. Across the street a couple walked hand in hand under the lights. A line had formed, waiting to get into the video studio.

"What is she like? What are her thoughts like?"

"Like a woman's."

"When will they be back?"

"Midnight tomorrow."

"I'll be here."

Ten of the older men were gathered in Jord Orlan's quarters. They sat stiffly and their eyes glowed. It had taken a long time for Jord Orlan to slowly bring them up to the proper pitch.

"Our world is good," he chanted.

"Our world is good," they responded in unison, the half-forgotten instincts rising up within them, hoarsening voices.

"The dreams are good."

"The dreams are good."

"And we are the Watchers and we know the Law."

"Yes, we know the Law."

Orlan held his arms straight out, his fists clenched. "And they would put an end to the dreams."

". . . an end to the dreams." The words had a sad sound.

"But they will be stopped. The two of them. The black-haired ones who are strange."

"They will be stopped."

"I have tried, my brothers, to show them the errors of their ways. I have tried to lead them into the ways of Truth. But they claim the three worlds are reality."

"Orlan has tried."

"I am not a vindictive man. I am a just man. I know the Law and the Truth. They have gone out into the noth-ingness, out into the emptiness that surrounds us, to look for the worlds of which we dream. Death will be a kind-ness."

"A kindness."

"Seek them out, my brothers. Put them in the tube of death. Let them slide down into the darkness and fall for-ever through the blackness. I have tried and I have failed. There is nothing else we can do."

"Nothing else."

They moved slowly toward the door, then faster. Faster. Jord Orlan stood and heard the pad of their feet against the warm floor, the growling in their throats. And they were gone. He sat down heavily. He was very tired. And he did not know if he had done the right thing. It was too late for doubts. And yet . . . He frowned. There was a basic flaw in the entire thought process. If outside was a nothingness, how could the two of them go outside and return? To have them do so would indicate that the nothingness was a "somethingness." And if that were true, then Raul Kinson's fanatic beliefs had to be given certain credence.

But once Raul Kinson was credited with any correct-ness, the entire structure of his own beliefs faded and dimmed. Jord Orlan's head hurt. It was a sad thing to have lived so long in perfect comfort with one's thoughts and then to have this tiny bitter arrow of doubt festering in his soul. He yearned to pluck it out. Possibly the spy had been mistaken. Possibly they did not go out into the nothingness.

He found himself descending toward the lowest level in great haste. He found the door. It did not take him long to remember the secrets of the twin wheels. He pulled the door open. And this time he dared to keep his eyes open. The wind whipped his cheeks. He squinted into it. The six ships stood tall against the huge red sun. Sand drifted in at his feet. He picked up a handful of it. He closed the door against the wind and leaned his forehead against the metal. He did not move for a long time. He turned and hurried back the way he had come.

Six of them were holding Raul. Raul's face was twisted with fury and, above the grunting of the captors, Jord Orlan heard the popping and crackling of Raul's shoulder muscles as he struggled, sometimes lifting his captors off their feet. Four of them were having an equally difficult time with the girl. They held her horizontally, two at her feet and two at her head. Her robe had been flung aside. As Jord Orlan neared them, they rushed with her toward the tube, toward the black oval mouth of it. But she twisted one foot free, planted it against the wall near the mouth of the tube and thrust with all her strength. They staggered and fell with her.

"Stop!" Orlan shouted.

"No!" the captors cried.

"Do you want their death to be easy? The tube is an easy death. Their sin is enormous. They should be thrust out into the emptiness outside to die there."

He saw doubt on their faces. "I order it!" he said firmly.

And, with Orlan leading, with the two captives no longer struggling, clad once more in robe and toga, the procession left the silent bystanders and went down to the door.

Orlan stopped the captors at the angle in the corridor. "Let them go on to the doorway alone. I shall go with them. If you look on nothingness it will forever blast your eyes and your mind. I will rejoin you when they have left."

They felt fear and anger, but fear was the stronger. They waited out of sight. Jord Orlan walked with Raul and Leesa.

He said, in a low tone, "I saw the odd garments. You need them to venture outside."

"What are you trying to tell us?" Raul demanded.

"That . . . there are things in our world that I do not understand. And before I die, I want to understand . . . everything. I did not believe the ships were there until I saw them with my own eyes. Now I share your sin. My belief has grown weak. If you could reach another world, then. . . ." He turned away. "Please hurry."

"Come with us," Leesa said.

"No. I'm needed here. If your heresies turn out to be true, my people will need someone to explain it to them. My place is here."

They left and he closed the door, retaining for a moment the image of the two figures leaning against the wind, the six ships in the background. He went back to those who waited and told them very calmly that it was all over.

FOURTEEN

THE LIGHT PLATES SET INTO THE CONTROL ROOM walls made a soft glow. Air came through the tiny grills in a sound like an endless sigh.

The entire control room was mounted on a shining piston that went straight down through the heart of the ship. The partitioned space along one wall, forty feet by ten, held the row of beds. Beyond the opposite partition were food stores, water tanks, sanitary equipment.

Leesa lay on the bunk and he folded the web straps

across her body, drawing them tight. The last strap circled
her forehead.

She looked up into his eyes. "Are we really ready?"

"We have to be. And I'll make a confession. If all this
hadn't happened, I was going to try it alone, without you."

"Maybe," she said softly, "this is all just another dream,
Raul. A more clever dream. Can you find Earth?"

"I know the number for Earth. I'll set it the way Bard
Lane explained. And then, quite soon, we'll know."

"Promise me one thing."

He looked down at her. "What is it?"

"If we are wrong. If there are no worlds out there. Or if
we lose our way, I want to die. Quickly. Promise?"

"I promise."

He slid the partition shut and went to the control panel.
His pilot's couch was on rails so that, once he was in
place, he could slide it forward under the vertical panel
and lock himself in place. He strapped his ankles and his
waist and pushed himself under to lie looking up at the
controls. He activated the three-dimensional screen. There
were the six ships, the tall white world, the sandy plain
and the hills. He opened the book and took a last look at
the reference number for Earth even though it had long
since been memorized. He set the ten-digit number, six
plus values and four minus ones, on the ten dials, checked
it again. The replica ship was in neutral position. Only
then did he strap the diaphragms firmly to his throat. He
pulled the headband up and tightened it, slid his arms
down into the straps.

And softly as he could, he made the vowel sound. The
ship shuddered, trembled. On the screen the tiny image
moved slowly upward, upward. Now the stern was as high
as the bows of the other ships. He strengthened the vowel
tone and the replica ship remained in the middle of the
screen, the planet moving away below it, the curvature beginning to show, the white tower world dwindling.

He rashly strengthened his tone once more. A vast
weight pressed his jaw open, punched down on his belly,
blinded him by pressing his eyes back into his head. He

heard, from a great distance, Leesa's scream of pain. He ceased all sound. The pressure slowly left him. He was dizzy with weightlessness. His home planet had shrunk to the size of a fist. It appeared in the lower right-hand corner of the screen and the image of the ship had dwindled until it was a bright mote against the darkening screen.

He took a weightless arm out of the strap, thumbed the knurled knob at the side of the screen. His planet slid off the screen and, by experimentation, he made the ship image grow larger. He moved close to it. The opposite knob seemed to rotate the ship itself end for end, but he realized that it merely shifted the point of vision. He adjusted it until he was looking forward from dead astern of the ship. The vast disc of the sun was straight ahead. He moved his hand to the replica ship and turned it through a ninety-degree arc to the right. As the sun slid off the screen, the replica ship moved slowly back to neutral. The screen showed distant spots of light against the utter blackness. He began to make the vowel sound again, cautiously at first, running it each time up to the limits of endurance, then resting in silence as the ship rushed, without noise, through the void. He understood that each time he made the sound he gave it another increment of speed. At last, no matter how loudly he made the sound, he could feel no answering downward thrust and he knew that the top limit had been reached.

Somewhere, ahead, the time setting would take effect. He did not know where. He did not know how long it would be.

FIFTEEN

FOUR MIDNIGHTS PASSED. BARD AND SHARAN WAITED three hours each time. The appointment was not kept. No thrusting fingers of thought entered their minds, singing gladly of reunion. For the first three midnights, Bard and Sharan were gay with each other, laughing too easily.

After the three tense hours of waiting had passed on the fourth night, Bard looked across the room at Sharan.

"He told me that their attitude was heresy in his world, Sharan."

"Why haven't they come? Why?"

"Logically we can make either of two assumptions. One, that they have been punished, perhaps put to death by their own people. Two, that they have started the voyage."

There were lines of strain around her mouth. "And the third possibility?"

"That it was a game they got tired of? That they have no ability to follow through on a course of action? Do you believe that, actually?"

Her smile was weak. "I guess not. Isn't it odd to feel that you know them so well, never seeing them?"

"Not so odd. Not with shared thoughts. Not with two . . . souls, if I can use that word, sharing the same brain tissue. Sharan, we owe them something. We owe them the assumption that they were forced, somehow, to start the trip. I don't know how long it will take. A month, possibly. Now just imagine what would happen if a ship of that description started to land here, or in Pan-Asia. Interceptor rockets would scream up. Shoot first and ask questions later. Our friends would be, within seconds, a large blue-white flash and a rain of radioactive particles. Have you thought of that?"

She put her hand slowly to her throat. "No! They wouldn't!"

"Look, Sharan. According to Raul and Leesa, the rest of the Watchers believe, even when they can visit three other planets through the dream machines, that they are alone in the universe. What is the primary egoism of man? That his planet is the only inhabited planet, his race the life-apex of the universe. Thus any unknown ship can *only* be the ship of an enemy nation on this same planet."

"Then they have no chance!"

"We are their chance, Sharan. We've got to let Earth know, somehow, that they are coming. They'll laugh at us. But even so, if Raul and Leesa are in transit, it might mean that at the crucial moment, someone may decide not to push the button. I wish they had come to us once more. I intended to warn them, tell them how to go into orbit outside the reach of the rockets and make identification. The way it stands they'll come directly in."

"If they never come, Bard?"

"We'll be the prize laughingstock of the century. Do you care?"

"Not really."

"We must start by giving the true story of the end of Project Tempo. We'll have to tell Bill Kornal first. Dr. Lurdorff will help us convince Bill. We've got to plant the story where it will get the maximum play from the press, radio, video, and everything else. That means that the four of us will have to put our cards, face up, in front of someone who not only can swing some weight around, but who has the sort of mind which might be receptive to this sort of thing. And Mr. X will have to have something to gain by carrying the ball. Any ideas?"

"It sounds like it ought to be somebody in government."

"Or how about a columnist with a big following. Let me see. Pelton won't do. I don't think we could sell it to Trimball."

"Say! How about Walter Howard Path? He has his column and the newscast on video. And he's the one that revived that ancient flying saucer business several years ago and claimed that the Air Force had never released the true data. He interviewed me, you know, after I walked out of that conference. He seemed nice, and the interview he published was at least a little bit friendly."

"I think he sounds like our boy, Sharan. There's the phone."

"So . . . so quickly?"

"How much time have we got to waste? Do you know?"

Sharan placed the call. It was almost four in the morning. Ten minutes later Walter Howard Path was on the line, speaking from his office-apartment in New York.

"Dr. Inly? Oh, yes. I remember you very well, Doctor."

"Mr. Path, would you care to have the exclusive story of what happened to Project Tempo?"

There was a long silence. "Dr. Inly, I wouldn't be terribly interested in it if it turns out to be some fairly tawdry little intrigue. The story wouldn't be good enough, and Tempo has been dead too long."

"Suppose I can show proof that Tempo was sabotaged by entities from another planet, Mr. Path?"

"Oh, come now, Dr. Inly!"

"Please hold the line. There is someone else here who wishes to speak to you."

Bard took the phone quickly. "Mr. Path, this is Bard Lane speaking. If you want to gamble on this story, I suggest you fly out here. We haven't too much time to waste. I know that superlatives are sometimes distasteful. But this, Mr. Path, is the biggest story of this or any other century."

"What is your address there?"

Walter Howard Path was a lean, enormously tall man with stooped shoulders, seamed cheeks and restless eyes. With his hands jammed in his hip pockets, he slouched over to the windows of the suite and looked down into the street. The four of them watched his motionless back. The conference lasted for five hours. Walter Howard Path had been angry at what he suspected was a ruse for one hour, incredulous for two more hours, grudgingly intrigued for the fourth hour, and obscurely frightened from then on.

Without turning he said, "It's a hell of a gamble, folks. Even when the fit is so good. Even when it answers so many questions about this crazy, violent planet of ours. Dammit, people won't *want* to believe a thing like that. And the ones who will jump into line will be the faddists, the cultists, the chronic end-of-the-world kids."

The tape recorder had been switched off. Walter Howard Path ambled back to the small table, fiddled with the tape reel.

He gave them all a weary smile. "So I guess I've got to hold my nose and go off the high board. Today is Wednesday. I'll blow it in the Sunday column and on the Sunday night program. We better dig us a hole and crawl in and hold our ears."

"This is Melvin C. Lynn, reporting the news for Wilkins' Mead and the Wilkins Laboratories, where the secret of your happiness was developed.

"Tonight, listeners, I am going to give you a different sort of news program. Today a colleague, Walter Howard Path, broke a rather astonishing story. It is considered ethical in this newscasting field never to run down a competitor directly. However, your Wilkins' Mead reporter feels that it is high time somebody took a lusty kick at Mr. Path's little red wagon.

"I have attempted to report the news to you honestly and sincerely. Sometimes I have fallen for a hoax. All of us have. But I have never been guilty of perpetrating one. Mr. Path has an enormous audience, far larger than mine. His responsibility to that audience is equally enormous. However, straight news reporting does not seem to satisfy our Mr. Path. You will remember his disinterment of the flying saucer hoax a few years ago. Possibly that sensationalism added a few more readers, a few more listeners.

"This time, however, Walter Howard Path has overreached himself. You all remember the scandal of Project Tempo. A Dr. Bard Lane, physicist, was dismissed for incompetence. He had shielded a technician, a William Kornal, who had committed sabotage on the project. There was a rumored intrigue between Dr. Lane and Dr. Sharan Inly, a sexy young psychiatrist on the project. In the finale debacle, twenty-eight persons died in the premature takeoff of the project ship. For honest reporters, there was no more news to be reported.

"Now let us examine what Walter Howard Path has

done. He has gathered around himself a very unwholesome little group. Dr. Bard Lane, discredited physicist. Dr. Sharan Inly, sexy psychiatrist. Mr. William Kornal, unpunished technician guilty of criminal sabotage. Dr. Heintz Lurdorff, hypnotist and alleged psychiatrist. Remember that with the possible exception of Lurdorff, the other three have every reason to find some sort of excuse for their previous actions.

"These five persons have cooked up the most fantastic story that ever hit these tired old ears. Long-range hypnosis from another planet! People like us who can come here on thought waves, or something, and make us do whatever they wish! Remind me to use those Martians or whatever they are as an excuse to my wife the next time I stay out too late. Now see how neatly it all fits. This is a wonderful country, listeners. No matter how crazy your story is, you can find somebody to believe you.

"Let us check and see the possible results, if Walter Howard Path is permitted to use the power of the press, radio and video to spread this new yarn of his. Dr. Bard Lane will, in the minds of fools, be acquitted of mismanagement, negligence and preoccupation with pretty Sharan instead of his job. Sharan Inly will become the high priestess of the new cult, and probably do very well indeed, financially. Dr. Heintz Lurdorff will get some publicity to trade on. William Kornal will be able to say, 'See? I didn't do it. Them Martians did it.'

"And how about Walter Howard Path? Priceless publicity on a story none of the rest of us would touch. Here is his master touch, though. He says that two of the alien people who grab us and make us do tricks are coming here in person, on a space ship, for goodness sake! A couple. Brother and sister. Raul and Leesa Kinson. Your Wilkins' Mead reporter wonders how long it took our Mr. Path to think up those names. Ever play anagrams? Take that name. Leesa Kinson. Use the letters in it. You can make two words. 'No sense.' With four letters left over, a-l-k-i, a practically prehistoric slang word for alcohol. How long is Walter Howard Path going to feed us delusions out of the bottom of a bottle? How brazen can his hoaxes become?

"Your Wilkins' Mead reporter leaves you with this one thought. How can a responsible video network or a responsible publisher give house room to an irresponsible man like Walter Howard Path and still claim to function in the public interest?"

"From the wires of the Associated Press. Yesterday morning one person was killed and three injured in a riot at Benson, Georgia. The clash was between the new cult which spends hours on hilltops watching for Walter Howard Path's mythical spaceships, and a detachment of the Georgia State Police. The new cult calls itself Kinsonians."

Excerpt from an address given at the annual dinner of the American Medical Association: "It is not altogether strange that the mass hallucination of the late nineteen forties involving 'flying saucers' should now be duplicated by a similar mass hallucination involving 'space ships.' Even the most cursory study of the history of mass hysteria shows clearly a cyclical pattern, with the outbreaks averaging twenty to forty years between peaks of intensity. At the latest count the 'space ship' which we are to play host to, according to the Kinsonians, has been reported landing at twenty-six different places. It is no accident that the locations of the 'landings' correlate most amusingly with the activity of the Kinsonian groups in those places."

POLICY DIRECTIVE 7112
PUBLIC RELATIONS SECTION, ARMED FORCES

1. As there is no desire to give special attention to unfounded charges regarding Project Tempo through any formal statement in rebuttal, all personnel are directed to refrain from commenting to representatives of the press.
2. All military personnel directly connected with Project Tempo have been given changes of sta-

tion to take them immediately outside the continental limits of the United States to new posts where the possibility of such interviews is lessened.

3. Official position on this matter, to be announced later, is that in the light of current world tension it is of dubious value to the national effort that mass hysteria should be whipped to such a peak that industrial absenteeism is at an unprecedented rate.

4. All officers and EM who profess publicly any degree of belief in Kinsonianism and, when warned, shall persist in such belief, will be considered unfit for duty.

"And now, ladies and gentlemen of the vidio audience, we bring you that lint-headed wonder of the stratosphere, that little man who *didn't* arrive in a space ship, that Yum-Bubble (Chew it, it's good for you) comic, Willy Wise! Hey, Willy! What's the matter, Willy? The cameras are over here, not up there on the ceiling."

"Don't bother me, Harry. I'm watching for that space ship. You want to make a million bucks, Harry?"

"That's the difference between you and me, Willy. I need a million bucks."

"Get another laugh and you'll need a job. Know what we ought to do? Put out some gunk to rub on your neck. I bet there are more cricks in more necks in this country than there are neckties."

"Willy, please look at the cameras. You've got a guest tonight. It's a she."

"Somebody else can watch for that ship. Hello, honey. What's your name?"

"Sharan Riley, Mr. Wise."

"Nice name, Sharan. I played Sharon, Pennsylvania, once. I killed 'em in Sharon. You got an aunt or a half sister or something named Sharan Inly?"

"Gee, no. She's famous."

"Say, I just got a theory, folks. How about this? You

ever see a good picture of that Sharan Inly? Here's how it all happened. She meets up with that Lane guy, see. She likes him. She wraps those lovely arms around his neck and . . . Bingo! Ever since that moment, folks, Dr. Lane has been seeing space ships, Martians and little green men. Who can blame the guy? Up until that point he probably never had his nose out of a Bunsen burner, or whatever they use in those labs."

"Today in Albany, at the request of Governor LePage, a bill was rushed through the state legislature making it illegal for anyone to make public speeches in favor of Kinsonianism. Critics claim that the bill is an infringement of the right of free speech. The governor defended his action on the grounds that the State of New York is suffering a curtailment of the supply of food, power and other necessary items, arising from the absenteeism of the Kinsonians. The governor claims that the Kinsonians seem to feel that the arrival of the alien space ship will somehow be synonymous with the end of the world. Other states will await, with interest, the decision of the courts on the legality of the new measure."

SIXTEEN

THE SUNDAY DUSK SLOWLY DARKENED THE STREET. BARD Lane turned from the window. The one suite had grown to two connecting suites. Bess Reilly had been found, and it did not take much encouragement to bring her back to work for Dr. Lane.

The phone on her desk rang constantly. Sharan and Lurdorff, using the octagonal cards, played quad-bridge on a lamp table. Kornal lay on the couch, his fingers laced over his stomach, peacefully asleep.

"What's the matter with them?" Bard demanded. "The

and down there in the street and just stare up at the win-
ows!"

Heintz Lurdorff grinned. "You must aggustom yourself
o being the high briest of what is bractically a new reli-
ion."

"It makes me nervous," Bard said. "And those phone
alls make me nervous. That woman who called up this af-
ernoon and called me the Anti-Christ. What was she talk-
ig about?"

"You are either the most honored or most detested man
n America, Bard," Sharan said. "I'll bid eleven spades,
Heintz."

"Always she geds all the gards," Heintz said dolefully.

"Anyway," Bard said. "We're doing it. We're doing
what we set out to do. I almost hate to think of what will
happen when and if that ship does set down. I don't know
why all this . . . took the public fancy so strongly. Do
ou know, Heintz?"

"Of gorse. Mangind has always wanted a whipping
boy. You gave them one. They love it. That governor of
Nevada, he has helped."

"Investigating the senseless murder cases and pardoning
people. I wonder."

Kornal yawned as he awakened. He looked at his
watch. "Nearly time for our favorite man, isn't it?"

Bard turned on the video. The screen brightened at
once. He turned off the sound while the commercial was
on, then turned the dial up as Walter Howard Path's an-
nouncer appeared on the screen.

". . . regret to announce that Walter Howard Path will
be unable to appear as usual. Mr. Path has suffered a
breakdown due to overwork and has been given an indefinite leave of absence. This program is being taken over by
Kinsey Hallmaster, distinguished reporter and journalist.
Mr. Hallmaster."

Mr. Hallmaster sat behind a vast desk and smiled im-
portantly at the video audience. With his twinkling eyes
and projecting front teeth he looked like a happy beaver.

"I am honored to be asked to take over this weekly

newscast. I am sorry, however, that Mr. Path cannot be wit
you as usual. He has my every hope for a speedy recovery

"My first duty is to read you a statement prepared b
Mr. Path.

" 'This is Walter Howard Path telling you that I hav
just received additional information regarding the spac
ship which has been alleged to——' "

"Alleged!" Bard shouted angrily. The others shushe
him.

" '——and these investigators, hired by me out of m'
own pocket, have brought me additional informatio
which now leads me to believe that I, as well as many o
the public, have been misled by Lane, Inly, Lurdorff an
Kornal. I have before me the notarized statement, amon
other things, of a tavern owner which states that for a pe
riod of three weeks Dr. Lane, in a consistently drunke
condition, gave speeches in his tavern regarding so-calle
mental visitations from space. I sincerely regret that I wa
taken in. There is no space ship. There are no Watchers
The alien brother and sister are figments of the overrip
imaginations of Lane, Inly, Lurdorff and Kornal. I say t
all of you who through an honest mistake have becom
Kinsonians, just mark it all up to the rather unusual gulli
bility of your reporter, Walter Howard Path.' "

Hallmaster put the document aside, folded his hands o
the edge of the desk. "There you have it," he said. "Mr
Path's health was broken by the discovery that he ha
been misled. I have a few other words to say about this en
tire matter, however. From an official and informed sourc
high in Washington, I have it on good authority that ther
is something far more sinister involved than the efforts of a
little clique of greedy people to make money out of bein;
in the public eye.

"We know, for an absolute fact, that Inly, Lane, Lur
dorff and Kornal were . . . shall we say, financially embar
rassed at a time two weeks before Mr. Path's unfortunat
backing of their wild tale. Now they are well enough of
to spend money freely, living in expensive hotel suites.

employing stenographic help. This money did not come from Mr. Path. Where did it come from?

"Now bear with me a moment. Suppose this nation were to be attacked. Interceptor rockets would flash up at the first target. But suppose that in advance we as a nation had been led to expect the arrival of some mythical space ship. Maybe the Kinsons will arrive in twenty simultaneous space ships which land in twenty industrial cities. Maybe their point of origin will not be some far planet, but rather the heartland of Pan-Asia. What then?

"Need I go further?"

For a jolly moment he let the implications settle into the minds of the vast audience. "And now for the more serious side of the news. We find that——"

Bard snapped off the set. The room was silent. The phone rang. Bess lifted it off the cradle and set it aside without answering it.

"That . . . low . . . dirty . . ."

"In five minutes," Sharan said softly, "he destroyed the whole thing, everything we've done. Every last thing."

"Maybe enough of them will still believe," Kornal said.

"After that?" Heintz Lurdorff said with a mild, dignified contempt. "I think now I go. I am sorry. There is nothing more we can do."

"The kiss of death, neatly administered," Sharan said. "Kissed off by a Wilkins' Mead culture. We need a new symbol. A monkey with six arms, like Vishnu, so he can simultaneously cover his eyes, ears and mouth."

"Give him one more hand, honey, so he can hold his nose," Kornal said.

After an hour on the phone, Bard Lane found out that Walter Howard Path was in a private sanitarium, committed by his wife, for an indefinite stay.

SEVENTEEN

AS CLOSELY AS RAUL COULD ESTIMATE, IT WAS TEN DAYS before the keening whine of a warning device startled them into immobility. They had been eating at the moment it sounded.

Leesa, startled, lost her grip on the wall railing and floated out beyond any chance of grasping it again. She writhed in the air, but could not appreciably change her position.

Raul calculated, pushed against the wall with his hand as he let go of the railing. As he passed Leesa he grasped her ankle and the two of them made one slow pinwheel in the air before touching the high railing on the opposite side of the cabin. He strapped her in, then made a slow shallow dive toward his own position. He arranged his own straps, slid forward into proper position, staring up at the panel.

Five long minutes passed before there was any change.

And then came an indescribable twisting. It was as though in one microsecond, vast hands had grasped him, turning as though wringing moisture from a bit of cloth, releasing him. Dimly he heard Leesa's startled cry. His vision cleared at once and he saw that the value of the first dial had returned to zero. A softer bell-note sounded, and he guessed that it meant an end to the warning period. Adjusting the screen he looked at strange star patterns.

Days later, when the warning sound came again, they strapped themselves in. The second time jump was like the first, but easier to bear because it was expected.

For the third, one day later, they did not go to position. They waited near the rail, and as the twisting came, her fingernails dug into his arm. He watched the convulsed look fade from her face as they smiled at each other.

An hour later the warning sound was more shrill. Again they went to their positions. One twisting, wrenching sensation followed closely on the heels of the next. When at last he was able to look at the dials, he saw that all of them had returned to zero. With a weakened hand he adjusted the image screen.

"Is . . . it over?" Leesa called.

"I think so."

"What do you see? Quickly!"

"Wait. I must turn the ship. Now I see a sun. Blazing white, Leesa."

"Their sun, Raul."

"I've seen their sun from Earth. It is yellow, Leesa."

"Look for the planet."

He turned the ship. A tiny distant planet was ghostly in the reflected sun glow.

"I see a planet!" he called.

"Take us there, Raul. Quickly. Oh, very quickly."

Cautiously he made the sound that drove the ship ahead, gave them weight after so many days. He felt the slick movement of the great cylinder which compensated in part for the force of the acceleration on their bodies. He made the sound again and the planet began to grow. He watched it grow, and it did not seem that he could breathe deeply enough.

And then he knew. He did not speak for a long time. He called to her and his voice was old.

"What is it, Raul?"

"The planet has nine moons, Leesa. Theirs has but one."

In the long silence he heard the muffled sound of her weeping. The planet grew steadily.

"Raul, are we still heading toward it?"

"Yes."

"Do you remember your promise?"

"I remember."

"Close your eyes, Raul. Do not touch the controls. It will be quick, Raul." Her voice had a curiously haunting quality, as though she were already dead.

He closed his eyes. Resignation. An end of struggle and rebellion. It would have been better to accept, to force belief in the warm, slow world of the Watchers. He thought of Earth. Possibly he had misread the metallic sheets, selected the wrong index. Out of so many millions of numbers, it could easily have been the wrong one.

Bard Lane and Sharan Inly would never be able to convince Earth that the Watchers existed. Just as he could not convince the Watchers that Earth was another reality, as true as their own.

He opened his eyes. The planet was alarmingly close. They were diving toward it. He closed his eyes again.

Someday maybe Earth would build such ships as this one. First they would go to the other planets of their own . . .

As the thought came he opened his eyes wide. He gave the replica ship a brutal twist and in the same instant the vowel sound. As the acceleration hammered him into unconsciousness he kept the thin impression of the face of the planet sweeping slowly off the screen.

In Bard Lane's dream he was back at Tempo watching the Beatty One rise into the arc of destruction. But this time the drive impetus was not steady. It came in hard flaring jolts that made the ship rise erratically on her suicide course. The dream faded and the jolting sounds turned to a heavy knocking at the door. He rubbed sleep-stuck eyes, rose painfully from his cramped position in the chair in which he had fallen asleep after Sharan had gone to bed.

"Coming, coming," he called with annoyance. He stretched and looked at his watch. Ten in the morning. The windows were gray, patterned with rain flung against them by a gusty wind. For a moment he could not remember why he felt so thoroughly depressed. And then he remembered Hallmaster's talk the night before.

He was in a completely foul mood when he yanked the suite door open. "Why didn't you just batter it down?" he said.

A thick-jowled man mouthing a cigar stub stood

planted in front of the door, two uniformed policemen behind him.

"Another minute and that's just what we would have done, friend," the man said. He walked flatfooted toward Bard, forcing Bard to step aside. The two policemen followed him into the suite.

"Maybe it would help if you tell me what you want," Bard said.

The jowled man knuckled his hat back off his forehead. "You're Lane." It was a statement of fact rather than a question.

"Nice of you to come and let me know so early on Monday," Bard said.

"I could learn to dislike you, friend." The stocky man turned and nodded at one of the two policemen. The uniformed man walked casually over and trod heavily on Bard's foot.

"Gee, excuse me," he said. He took his weight away, trod heavily on the other foot. Bard's fist swung automatically, all the strain and heartache and disappointments of months erupting into a rage that was like ice.

The policeman partially blocked the blow, but it slipped off his forearm and landed on the heavy cheekbone with a satisfying crack.

The two policemen moved in with deft efficiency and pinned both of Bard's arms. The jowled man took the cigar from his mouth and rolled it between his fingers.

"It was reported to me, Dr. Lane, by the management of this hotel, that you were acting strangely. I am Hemstrait, the health officer. I came here to investigate the report and find that it was true. You attacked Patrolman Quinn without provocation."

"Just what do you want?"

"I don't want anything. I'm committing you to the state hospital for sixty days of observation and treatment. Nuts like you can't run around loose."

"Whose orders are you following, Hemstrait?"

The man had the grace to blush. "Hell, Lane. They'll do you some good out there. Where's the Inly woman?"

"You don't need her too."

"The hotel says that she's crazy too. I got a job to do. I got to investigate all reports."

At that moment Sharan, flushed with sleep, a white robe belted around her, opened the bedroom door and came out. "Bard, what is——" She stopped and her eyes widened as she saw Bard being held.

"You let him go!" she said.

"Lady, you're irrational," Hemstrait said.

"Don't say or do anything," Bard said quickly.

Hemstrait gave Bard a look of annoyance. He moved close to Sharan, rested a beefy hand on her shoulder. She shrugged it off. He replaced it. She moved away. He followed her, grinning. She cracked her palm off his thick cheek. He grinned and grabbed her. "Lady, as health officer I'm committing you to the state hospital for sixty days of observation and treatment. You ought to know better than to attack the health officer."

"It's no good, Sharan," Bard said in a bleak tone. "Somebody gave him his orders. The same people who took care of Path, probably. And gave Hallmaster that paper to read. We're a disturbing influence."

"Shut up, friend," Hemstrait said jovially. "Come on, lady. They'll be good to you out there. We picked up Lurdorff and Kornal in the lobby this morning. Kornal made such a fuss we had to put him in a jacket. Now you people are going to be more sensible than that."

On the following Wednesday morning, Sharan Inly, clad in the gray shapeless hospital garment, was taken by a matron-attendant to the office of the young state psychiatrist. The matron waited behind Sharan's chair. The psychiatrist was a thin-faced young man with an earnest, dedicated look.

"Dr. Inly, I'm very happy to meet you. I had hoped that when we did meet, it would be under . . . more pleasant circumstances. I particularly remember some of your papers that appeared in the Review."

"Thank you."

"I know that you must be interested in your own case

An unusually persistent delusion and, what is more startling, a shared delusion. Most unusual. And, as you may be aware, an unfavorable prognosis." He hitched himself uncomfortably in the chair. His smile was wan. "Usually I have to explain to the patient the implications of deep shock. Of course, you worked with Belter when he was perfecting the technique. . . ."

His voice trailed off.

Sharan fought the fear back. She made her voice calm. "Isn't that treatment a bit extreme in this case, Doctor? Memory patterns never return. That means complete reeducation from mindlessness, and sufficient damage so that on the Belter Scale, intelligence never goes beyond the DD level."

"Frankly," he said, "it makes me feel uncomfortable to prescribe it in the case of this delusion the four of you share. Dr. Lurdorff grew quite violent. He will be treated this afternoon. A shame, actually. So brilliant a mind . . . but misdirected, of course. All of you can be turned into productive members of society. You'll be quite capable of leading a satisfying life, of doing routine work. And you know how we've speeded up reeducation. Speech is adequate in a month. Incontinence ends in a week."

"May I ask if a consulting psychiatrist can be called in, Doctor?"

"Oh, this treatment is the result of consultation, Dr. Inly. Very good men. Now, outside the delusionary cycle, you are quite capable of making decisions. With the nonviolent cases it is policy here to give you time to write letters, make wills, dispose of property, that sort of thing. We'll give you false memory of a different life, a new name, a slightly altered face. You'll be sent, of course, to one of the critical labor areas, and a competent social worker will get you started."

"Actually, it's death, isn't it?"

"Now let us not be emotional, Dr. Inly. I had hoped that as a psychiatrist and a neuro-surgeon, you would——"

Sharan forced a smile. "I guess it's time for confession,

Doctor. We all thought up this Watcher business as a publicity thing. We all needed money."

He shook his head sadly. "Surely you know better than that! Such a perfectly standard reaction, Dr. Inly. Under induced hypnosis you all clung to every single phase of the shared delusion."

"A question then. If a delusion can be shared, possibly it isn't a delusion."

He chuckled, at ease for the first time in the interview. "You people! Don't you see that basically it's a desire for escape? The world as you know it has become unbearable for the four of you. Too bad you didn't recede into a catatonic state. We could have treated that. Instead you invent a delusionary race on a far planet on which you can blame your own inadequacies. Dr. Inly, we are the only race in the universe. Anything else is a dream. The only reality is here. And we must accustom ourselves to live with it, unpleasant as it may be, or else be treated by someone who can make the world bearable to you by some artificial means."

"And you, Doctor, are a blind, simpering, egocentric fool."

He flushed. "I have too much sympathy for you, Dr. Inly, to permit you to anger me. Use a long view. You are a healthy young woman. Dr. Lane is a sturdy man. Your validity from now on will be in work units for society and in the bearing of children. I was prepared to reeducate the two of you as a family unit. It would be interesting to see what degree of devotion could be induced. That choice, of course, is up to you and Dr. Lane. I shall see him next."

"It doesn't matter," Sharan said tonelessly. "It won't be . . . me. I shall be dead. You forget, Doctor, that I worked with deep shock techniques. I have seen that . . . mindlessness."

"Then I shall tell Dr. Lane that you are willing. We'll be ready for the two of you tomorrow morning. The attendant will arrange legal help for you, and see that you have writing materials."

Sharan turned at the door and tried to speak to him again. The young doctor was making notations on her file. He did not look up. The attendant urged her into the hall with gentle force.

Bard Lane stood in the hall with two guards, waiting. His face was gray. He looked at her and did not seem to recognize her. Sharan did not speak to him. Sharan Inly would never speak to Bard Lane again. Two strangers would speak to each other, and that was no longer important.

EIGHTEEN

IT IS A PLEASANT THURSDAY MORNING IN OCTOBER OVER most of the country. One high is static over most of the Gulf Coast. Another is apparently anchored in the Chicago area. The Secretary of Weather is conferring with Agriculture on the advisability of securing Canadian permission to dissipate the front building up in the northwest.

An Atlanta hostess decides to continue the party that started Wednesday afternoon. She stirs guests out of their stupor, smilingly hands them the amphetamine cocktails which will bring the gaiety back to life.

A bemused broker shivers in the web seat of his helicycle as he laboriously forces it above its operational ceiling, hoping that the Air Police won't intercept him until he is quite ready to loosen the strap and take the long, long drop into the corduroy canyons of the city far below.

Timber Mulloy, sullen and hung over, leads his protesting musicians through an early-morning practice session for a new visi-tape album which may bring in enough royalties to catch up on back alimony payments.

At Fonda Electric seven hundred girls are waiting for the ten A.M. cigarette break.

A teen-age heiress in Grosse Point stands nude before her full-length mirror and cuts her throat with a hard, ripping pull of her right hand and wrist.

In an isolated radar station, Major Tommy Leeber stares at his tarnished major's leaf and curses the day he was selected as aide by General Sachson. Sachson, a continent away, stands in front of a steel mirror and carefully clips gray nostril hairs while he thinks of the two years before he can retire.

Sharan Inly lies face down on her cot, waiting for them to come for her. On the other side of the building Bard Lane sits on his cot, slowly leafing through the memories that will be taken from him.

It is a pleasant morning.

In Connecticut a sanitarium attendant is being cursed by his superior for not finding Walter Howard Path in time to save his life.

It is thirty seconds after ten o'clock. Seven hundred girls are striking matches and clicking lighters.

Twelve miles from Omaha, a radar-radak technician frowns as he studies the pip on his screen. He adjusts for a new focus, and, as he puts the track on automatic, he runs his eye down the list of EXP flights. On automatic track the height, speed, and direction appear below the screen.

Speed is a constant. Direction almost due south. Altitude decreasing at the rate of a half mile a second.

His next moves are deft and quick. He punches the station alarm button, then throws open the switch which sounds the alarm instantaneously in twelve interceptor stations and puts them in direct communication with his board.

A nurse lays out the salve to be applied to temples and electrodes. The technician checks the dials on the shock equipment. The young state psychiatrist shuts the door of his room behind him and walks down the hall without haste.

Alert is flashed to interception points. Five more screens pick up the image and tie in the interception sta tions. Rocket tubes, six hundred of them, ten at each interceptor station, are so tied in with the automatic track on the screens that they point, unerringly, at the proper interception point in the predicted track of the screen pip. If the pip had been shown as coming straight down, manual control of firing would have been automatically cut out. No human hand could have moved quickly enough.

At the master control station SW, outside El Paso, a hard-faced colonel cuts out all manual control at the interceptor points, and takes over the decision. There are six buttons under his fingers. Each one discharges one full ten-round from the designated interceptor point.

The mike is close to his lips. He watches the screen. "Course change," he says in a flat tone. His words boom loudly in a small room in Washington. The small room is beginning to fill rapidly. "Velocity down one half. Target now heading straight up. Continuing loss of velocity. Either unmanned with defective controls, or manned incompetently."

The speaker above the colonel's head says, metallically, "Intercept when we get a predicted course toward any critical area."

A major standing near the colonel says, "This will give the Kinsonians a bang."

The colonel doesn't answer. He is thinking of his son, of the eruption of crazy, bloody, irrational violence that had ruined his son's life. His iron face does not change. He remembers the voice of Walter Howard Path.

"New direction north-northwest. Altitude three hundred thirty miles. Within range. Velocity down to five hundred miles per hour. Altitude three hundred, velocity four seventy."

"Intercept," the speaker says.

Taut fingers poise over the buttons.

"Intercept," the speaker says. "Acknowledge."

Twenty-five years of discipline balanced against the memory of the stunned, uncomprehending look on the face of a boy.

"Recommend stranger be permitted to land."

He hears the major's taut gasp, sees the major's hand reaching to punch the buttons. He turns and smashes his fist against the major's jaw.

Flat, emotionless voice. "Believe stranger preparing to land Muroc."

Video in the lounge at Fonda Electric. Radio in the room where amphetamine is working its frantic magic in Atlanta. Music from the pocket pack in the broker's pocket, faint against the hard roar of the wind as he tumbles over and over, down and down. Timber Mulloy, taking a breather, tuning in to hear one of his own records. Bedside radio in Grosse Point singing softly to something at the base of a full-length mirror. Radio playing soothingly on the desk of the floor nurse as a young psychiatrist walks toward the shock room, passing the desk . . .

". . . We interrupt this program to inform America that, at this moment, a space ship of unknown origin is attempting a landing at Muroc. The ship answers the description given by Lane to Walter Howard Path in what was believed to be a hoax. Word has just been received that the first attempt at landing was unsuccessful. Further news will be reported as soon as received. We now return you to the network programs in process."

Jord Orlan left the case of dreams and returned to his chambers. He had bitten through his lower lip and the taste of blood sickened him.

He sat alone and tried to rebuild something in which he could no longer believe. A structure had collapsed in his mind, and the shards of it were useless.

He saw, in memory, the great ship, its ancient hide pocked by space fragments, sitting on the surface of an alien world. Outside, where there had been six ships, there were now five.

He had slid into the mind of a spectator, and he had seen Raul and Leesa taken in a vehicle from the side of the ship to a distant building. He had seen them, in one of the dreams, thinner than they had been when they left. At one point he had moved close enough to hear Raul

peak, his voice thin with strain, yet exultant, speaking
he Earth language awkwardly, clumsily because he was
speaking from memory alone.

"The Doctor Inly and Doctor Lane. It is them we must
see quickly."

There was nothing left to believe. And he remembered
the Law. Such travel meant an end to the dreams. He
saw, ahead of him, the long empty years, full of nothing
but the games that were now pointless.

He knew what he had to do. He found a heavy tool in
the lowest level. By the time he had finished what he had
to do, his hands were raw and blistered.

And he went down to his people to tell them that the
dreams had come to an end.

NINETEEN

SHARAN STOOD BESIDE BARD LANE. THEY STOOD CLOSE
together and looked through the glass wall of the studio.
Raul and Leesa sat behind a table, the cameras focused on
them, the interviewer at the end of the table. With the help
of Bard and Sharan, Raul and Leesa had won the right to
dress as the people around them, rather than in the conspic-
uous style of the Watcher colony.

"How long is this going to go on?" Sharan asked wea-
rily.

"It will go on just as long as they are the only two out-
siders on this planet. That sort of novelty will never wear
off."

"So you better hurry with Tempo Two, my friend, and
go grab off some people from Marith and Ormazd. How
is it going?"

"Good, now that the Pan-Asia group decided to come
in on it. They're still a little wary of our generosity in giving them access to the whole works."

Sharan looked at Leesa through the glass. "She's very patient, isn't she?"

"She explained that to me. It's a sort of . . . penance you might say. For what she has done in the past, what her people have done. How do you like her English?"

"Not anywhere near as quaint as it was, at least." Sharan giggled. "Know what I remember, Bard? The time you described her as probably being bald and built like a twelve-year-old child."

Bard Lane remembered too. He looked at the slim, delicate, dark-haired girl. She met his glance and made a small shrug of patience. He said, "She told me that on her world she was considered some sort of a brute-woman. Here she's just a pretty girl who looks a bit more fragile than the average. And your Raul could lose himself in any crowd."

"He could not!"

Bard grinned. They listened to the closing minutes of the program. "Now, Mr. Kinson, you say that the Watchers have not contacted you or your sister in any way during the weeks you have been here with us."

Raul frowned. "I do not understand that. I do not see why they have not done so. It would be so easy."

"Now I have something that may come as a surprise to both of you. We have just received tabulated data from all law enforcement agencies covering the time you have been here. There has been an unprecedented drop in crimes of violence. Violence is still with us, of course. Until we learn the secrets of that other world you told us about, it will probably always be with us. But motiveless violence, inexplicable actions—they seem to have gone way down."

Bard saw Leesa and Raul stare at each other, say a few swift words in their own tongue.

Leesa said, "It would seem then, that either they know and understand now, or they are not using the dream machines. We do not know which. We will only know when someone goes . . . back."

"Would you like to go back?"

She turned her head slowly so that she looked directly at Bard. Her chin lifted a bit and her eyes softened. "In my life, sir, I go nowhere without the Doctor Lane."

Sharan said, "My, my! How you can blush!"

"Hush."

"And you, Mr. Kinson? Will you go back if you have a chance?"

Raul frowned. "I do not know if I can say this well. It is a plan, and a part of the big Plan I told you about. Now the dreamers are not destroying. The three planets my ancestors colonized can join together. This Earth can give Marith much. But Earth and Marith can get most from Ormazd. We are three children, going different ways, now grown to strength with which each can help all.

"Now with my plan, and I mean for me as a person, as you know I have taken to wife the Doctor Inly in line with your customs, the same as my sister and Doctor Lane in that ceremony you made us do before cameras so all could see. Now I am saying too blunt, which goes against your custom. None of you watching this can know each other, in your hearts. Even now I do not know well the Doctor Inly, though married. Not as well as when, with the dream machines, I entered her mind to know it as my own. It is the same with my sister. We have talked. We are not as happy as we could be, because of the barrier between us.

"In dreams of Ormazd I learned that they can use the minds at close range the way the dream machines did over vast distances. It is there that I would go and my sister would go, with the two we have married. And there Ormazd can teach us this thing which is necessary if a person is not to be . . . forever a little apart and a little bit lonely.

"When it is learned by the four of us, we wish to come back and teach others. That way the rest of that violence which you told me can be also taken away from this planet. It is . . . a dream and a good one this time. For a long time the three planets of the children of the Leaders

of long ago have waited for the time of reuniting, for th
time of progress that is to come.

"All of this will be slow, I think. The biggest change
will not come in the life of any of us who are here or you
who listen. But for myself, I want that small chang
which gives mind freedom to enter mind as soon as I can
have. See, I do not speak well yet.

"To have this come about, I wish to be with my wife.
wish to work with the Doctor Lane. There are things
can learn and things I can do. I wish no longer to be an
animal to be looked at with those camera things. My sis
ter does not like this camera thing either. Now we wish to
go to work on that very great ship which, we hope, wil
carry part of the name of a man who was good and wis
and very brave."

He smiled into Sharan's eyes.

"That ship, it is to be called Pathfinder," he said softly

AFTERWORD

I wrote *Wine of the Dreamers* in 1950 and
Ballroom of the Skies the following year.

When Knox Burger, who edits my work at Fawcett
Publications, suggested we resurrect these two books,
the only science fiction novels I have ever published, I
read them for the first time since the obligatory reading
in galley proofs nearly twenty years ago.

It would be a meretricious idiocy for any writer with
any respect and consideration for his following to foist
upon them the creative mistakes of the early years. I have
closets full of previously published stories which will
never see print again, regardless of whether I am on the
scene or off in that limbo which I suspect is reserved
for all novelists—where we are condemned to lie for half
of eternity in tiny rooms with the creatures of our own
devising.

Though it may be merely one more symptom of the
writer's flawed objectivity, I found both these novels to be
more cohesive and provocative than I had expected.

I have not revised them. I ached to doctor much
stilted conversation, but to do so would have been to cheat,
as somehow the pretentious and overly grammatic
speeches made by the actors are touchingly typical of
the genre.

They are both more accurately categorized as science
fantasy than as science fiction, in that they are neither

173

space-adventure, nor mad-scientist, nor doom-machine epics.

The two novels are companion pieces in that they provide two congruent methods of accounting for all the random madness and unmotivated violence in our known world, and two quite different answers as to why, with all our technology, we seem unable to move a fraction of an inch toward bettering the human condition and making of life a universally more rewarding experience.

This, for the writer, is the charm of such novels, as they enable him to step up onto a small shaky soapbox and say something, without ever lecturing the reader, about the moral and emotional furniture of our lives. Books of this sort have a functional relationship to the world's religions, in that they also make a sober attempt to explain the inexplicable, account for the unaccountable

I confess to being particularly jolted by finding in *Wine of the Dreamers* that the Paris Peace Talks were still going on in 1975, that the Asians were quarreling with Russia about the orbits for snooper satellites, and that a substance was being advertised and sold to millions of Americans as a non-alcoholic, non-habit-forming beverage which would heighten the sensory response to such stimuli as a kiss or a sunset. I wish I could have equivalent prescience in personal matters.

To those of my reader-friends who are turned off completely by these organized speculations and term them "silly," I extend apologies. I am glad to have these back in print. I suspect, however, that those who cruise vicariously aboard *The Busted Flush* with one T. McGee—as do I—will find things in these books which will reward and amuse.

Herein there are no bug-eyed monsters, except the ones forever resident in the human heart. There are no lovelies being rescued by space explorers from giant insects who talk in clicks and carry distintegrators. No methane atmospheres. Nothing emerging from the evil swamps. Not even a single dutiful robot, harboring either electronic love or the cross-wired circuitry of rebellion. Because of these omissions I may well be responsible, also, for turning off the hard-core aficionado of science fiction who, because these are more about people than things, might also term them "silly."

My most signal satisfaction in rereading these two novels, and in authorizing their reappearance, was to discover that I had not, as I had suspected, sacrificed story to message. They move right along. It had been so long since I had written them that my recall was fogged by fifty intervening novels. And so I had much ironic amusement in finding myself, for the first time, reading my own work with considerable curiosity as to what would happen next.

JOHN D. MACDONALD

Sarasota, Florida
September 1968

ANOTHER SCIENCE FICTION CLASSIC BY THE
AUTHOR OF THE TRAVIS McGEE SERIES

BALLROOM
OF THE SKIES

Have you ever stopp d to wonder why the world is eternally
war-torn? Why men of good will, seeking only peace, are
driven relentlessly to further disaster?

In **Ballroom of the Skies** John D. MacDonald suggests a strange
and monstrous explanation. He pictures an intricate and totally
convincing future society, where India rules the globe, and
everyone chases the mighty rupee. The First Atomic War has
just ended, and already the Second is clearly building.

People shrug. War is man's nature, they think. And that's what
Dake Lorin thought until he became aware of the aliens living
among us—and discovered their sinister purpose.

R1993   *A Fawcett   Gold Medal Book*   60¢

wherever paperbacks are sold